Memorizing Mace © 2020 by
All rights reserved.
Published by Larken Roman
Cover by Elizabeth Mackey Designs

Memorizing Mace (Twist Brothers Book Two)

He's the bounty hunter who destroyed her life. She's the cop out for revenge.

Loralei

The last person I wanted to see after losing part of my memory was Mace Twist.

The cocky jerk betrayed me in the worst possible way, and I vowed I'd never give him another chance.

But he's the only one who can help me reconstruct my missing memories, so I'm forced to team up with my sexy nemesis.

As hard as I try to forget the blazing passion we once shared, my body has him memorized.

Can I take what I need from him without losing my heart all over again?

Mace

I rescued Loralei from kidnappers, but she's still in danger.

She lost her job, there's a bounty on her head, and no one is standing up to take her back.

We've danced on the line between love and hate for a long time, but now she needs my protection.

I'll do what it takes to keep her safe, but I can't promise I'll keep her out of my bed.

If you like enemies to lovers with bad boy alpha-male heroes and kickass heroines, you'll love Memorizing Mace.

"Love is not how you forget. It's how you forgive."

Chapter 1 Loralei Valentine

Mace

My hands twitch as the glow of lights on the helicopter launch pad come into view.

This will be a story retold around the Twist family campfire for generations. History in the making. Tonight Arthur Morganna's reign of terror ends.

Cutter, my best friend and brother, has captured his abusive biological father alone on an island off the coast and has called us in for back up. This is what I live for. There's no better way to spend a Saturday night than delivering justice to a predator like Morganna. He hurt my family, now we hurt him.

I hop out of my truck and hold my arms out wide as I walk toward the four people waiting for me. "I'm here now. The ass kicking may commence."

My younger brother Remy rolls his eyes and frowns. "This is no joke, Mace."

"I'm serious. Crank her up." I lift my chin toward his luxury private helicopter. He spent ten million dollars on that hunk-a-junk, and hasn't taken me for a ride yet. "Show me your new bird."

He shakes his head as we share our fist-bump-bro-hug greeting. He turns and climbs in, prepping her for take off. From what I can see, the inside looks sweet. Leather seats, conference table. We're flying in style tonight.

My adopted father walks up to greet me with the family handshake and an extra hard smack on the shoulder. "Glad you could make it, Mace."

"Dropped everything and broke the sound barrier to get here in time." We keep our grip locked as we make eye contact. I'm hard to nail down, but for family, I always come through.

My mom and my sister Sutton are the last two people to say hello to me. They're dressed to kill. Skinny black jeans, dark leather jackets, hair pulled back, red lipstick on serious faces. "You guys look badass tonight."

I have to bend down to enfold my mom in a hug. Sutton's not much of a hugger, so we just do the fist bump. "I'm so nervous." She wrings her hands together.

"Don't worry. We got this." She stays out of the fray most of the time, but this one is personal. Morganna abused her too when she was young, so she wants to be there tonight.

"You ready, Ma?"

My mom pulls her shoulders back and forces a tentative smile. "Let's do it."

We all climb on Remy's posh chopper, the rotors boot up, and the Twist family is off the ground. History, here we come.

***

I can't sit still during the flight over the Pacific Ocean to Little Santa Rosa Island. It's only forty minutes, but feels like hours. Miles of dark waves with no sign of human activity have me doubting we'll ever find it. If we're late, I might miss out on all the action. Cutter has first dibs on Morganna, but if there's anything left of him, I'm taking my turn.

"There it is." Remy points to a cluster of lights ahead.

We're all staring out the windows, trying to catch a glimpse of what's happening down there. Palm trees blow in the ocean wind and a geometric white building draws all of our attention. Finally, as we touch down next to another helicopter, I see Cutter standing outside with Cass, blood smeared on his clothes, eyes wide, shoulders stiff like he's in shock. Cass is holding her arm, her hair is whipping in the wind, but they look okay. Another woman with them appears equally shocked, but uninjured.

Damn. Looks like we missed it. I'm happy they're okay, but would've liked to see it all go down.

I don't wait for the propellers to slow before jumping out the door. My parents and sister follow behind me.

The noise mutes their words, but my dad helps Cutter move Cass and the other girl out of the wind and into seats in the helicopter. My mom opens her first aid kit and starts checking Cass right away.

Cutter hugs Sutton for a long time. Sister and brother finally facing down their abuser. "Morganna's dead," Cutter says with the finality of a man who's been through hell and come out victorious on the other side.

Well, that answers that question. He's dead. Cutter took care of him. Good. The man terrorized Cutter and Sutton for years. He's the one responsible for the scars on his back and his heart. I'm glad he's gone. Still wanted to see it, but the deed is done. "Good job, brother."

He shakes his head like he feels bad, but he shouldn't. That asshole deserved to die. "Anyone else inside?" I ask as I hand my brother his gun.

"I don't know. It's a crime scene. Don't go in there," Cutter replies.

"I won't touch anything." I draw my weapon and jog to the front door of the structure. Cutter attempts to call me back, but he knows I can't be stopped once I'm in motion.

Inside, the living room is lit up but empty. All the bedroom doors in the east corridor are open. No one inside.

On the west side, I wince when I find Morganna's slashed up body on the floor in one of the rooms. Cutter did a number on him. He's motionless in a halo of blood. Must've been fun to watch.

Next room over is locked. I kick it open. A lifeless woman lies on the carpet, needles on the bed. She's barefoot, her jaw hanging slack, dark hair covering her face. "Oh shit." My heart, which was already racing, takes off at a million miles a second. I stand over her for a beat, not sure if I should touch her. It is a crime scene like Cutter said, but if she's not dead, she needs help right away. She has a slow pulse when I check her neck. Her chest rises and falls ever so slightly. She's alive.

I scoop up her limp body and start running. Her head flails, but I have to hurry to get her safe.

Lots of shocked eyes stare back at me when I run up to the helicopter. "There were needles on the bed," I say to my mom. I'm out of breath and not sure what to do. She could die in my arms if we don't act fast.

My mom pats her cheek. "Hello. Can you wake up for me?" No response.

This is not good. My mom and Remy share a serious look and burst into action. "Put her on the seats."

It doesn't feel right to let her go, so I sit down with her in my lap. She could be someone's daughter, sister, wife. If she were mine, I wouldn't want her dying alone, I'd want someone to hold her, so I'm doing that.

I press her cheek against my chest and move her hair out of the way. My stomach pitches to my toes when I see her face. Instantly, I know her. I know this girl.

I've known her for a long time.

How could she be here? Why? She was fine last time I saw her. More than fine, she was radiant. I even followed her around for a while and didn't see any signs of trouble.

My mom gives her a nasal shot of some anti-overdose drug Remy had stored in the first aid kit. She heaves and coughs. Her eyes open briefly then close again. She's breathing, and she can open her eyes. That's a good sign.

"I know her." My voice is hoarse as everyone else looks on.

"You know her?" my mom asks. "What's her name?"

I can't believe it's true. It's impossible. I check her face again to make sure.

"Loralei. Her name is Loralei Valentine."

They all freeze when I say it. They know her name. She's caused us a lot of grief over the years as she attempted to exact revenge against me by hurting my family. Cutter and Remy hate her. Technically, I'm supposed to hate her too for what she did, but the past is so completely irrelevant now as she clings to life. This can't be happening to her.

"What the hell was she doing in there?" I yell at Cutter.

He shakes his head. "I didn't even know she was here."

"Let's get her to a hospital," my mom says.

They start talking about something, but my head spins. I can't concentrate on their words. It's a jumble of noise, and we haven't left the ground yet.

"Hurry!" My urgent yell stops everyone short. "We need to get her some help. No more talking."

Cutter and Cass rush to climb out of the helicopter. "Where're you going?"

"We're staying here to talk to the authorities." Cutter takes Cass's hand. "We'll check in with you later."

"Fine." I nod, but I don't care what anyone else does right now. I need her at the hospital, getting help, making sure she keeps breathing. I rub my thumb over pallid skin on Loralei's inanimate cheeks. She's ice cold. "Let's go."

Finally, my dad closes the door, the rotors ramp up with a thumping buzz, and we hover above the ground for a second.

Remy lifts the helicopter from the pad, and we pivot across the Pacific toward home.

I wanted action, but not this kind. Never this.

She can't die. Not her. Not Loralei.

"Hold on, sweetheart. We're getting you some help."

Chapter 2 Mace Twist

Loralei

Stinging light blinds me through my squinted eyes. Slowly, perforated ceiling tiles above my head come into focus. Where am I? My chest feels numb, but my arms and legs are burning.

"What the hell was she doing there?" In the distance, a deep angry voice rumbles and echoes, but the pounding in my head muffles it. "There's no way she went there on her own. Giselle and Arthur must be behind this."

The voice is definitely speaking to someone else. It seems like he could be talking about me, but I have no idea what the words mean. As I wake up more fully and turn my head, I see I'm in a hospital room. Panic bubbles in my chest. I'm in the hospital? And someone is yelling on their phone? What the heck?

"This is driving me nuts. She needs to wake up and answer some damn questions. First she shows up at Twist Cabins and causes a brawl. A few weeks later, she's unconscious on Morganna's island?" He pauses. "How could I have missed this? I'm telling you, I followed her to see what she was up to. She was clean. No ties to you or Morganna, so I let her be. I shoulda stayed on her."

He's quiet for a moment while I try to process all that's been said.

Twist Cabins.

I did go to Twist Cabins, but that wasn't weeks ago. It was just a day or two ago. I didn't realize someone there figured out I was behind the gossip that caused a massive fight to break out.

So whoever this person is, he was there, he recognized me, and he followed me.

Oh no.

Tell me it's not him. It can't be him.

"How's Cass's arm?" The voice sighs and grunts as he listens to the other end of the conversation.

My eyes adjust and finally focus on a dark figure sitting in the corner of the room. Head down, long legs covered in dark jeans, thighs wide with his muscular forearms braced on them. One hand is buried deep in the curly long hair that conceals his face, but the visceral burst of dread rushing through me tells me exactly who he is.

It's him.

Mace Twist. My arch enemy since I was eighteen. The thief who stole my virginity then used me to get to my father. God, I hate him and he hates me.

Now he's sitting in a hospital room with me ranting about nonsensical things. Suddenly, it's hard to breathe, and I have to look away from the disturbing sight to put this all together. Okay. Let me think. It's so hard through the headache, but Mace is here. I'm in a hospital room. He saw me at Twist Cabins two days ago, and now he's angry at me for being on an island I've never heard of.

Oh Lord. What have I gotten myself into this time?

Mace grunts and shakes his head. "It's time for you to drop this now, Cutter. He's dead."

I hold back the gasp that wants to fly from my lips. Someone's dead? Cutter is Mace's older brother. Have I woken up in some kind of Twist Brothers' nightmare?

Mace must be so deep in his conversation that he hasn't realized I've woken up. He huffs out an ironic laugh. "I think she's the one woman in the world I can't persuade."

If he's talking about me, he's right. The hypnotizing power he wields over other women to persuade them to give up their values won't work on me. Not again.

"I'll ask her about Giselle, but I got work to do. I'm just here till she wakes up then I'm gonna make myself scarce."

So his plan is to leave once he knows I'm awake?

"Will do. Peace out."

He ends the call and looks up from under his sun-kissed hair. His face is tan from surfing even though it's winter. The man I've always thought of as the Hawaiian Jesus is sitting in a hospital room with me. His deep blue stare sears my eyes. The same gaze that seduced me then destroyed my life. He's dangerous. He can hurt me. Fear squeezes my chest and panic bubbles up my throat. This is unsafe. I need to run.

I scramble out of the bed, but I'm connected to tubes that shake and tug my arm back.

"Hey, hey, hey. Easy." He stands up and walks toward me with his palms down like he's herding a lost calf.

"Where the hell am I?" My voice comes out unusually fast and high-pitched.

"You're at SF General." He remains calm which only freaks me out further.

"Why?"

"We found you unconscious on Arthur Morganna's island." His brow furrows and his voice is solemn, but he can't be serious.

I don't even know Arthur Morganna. I've heard of the famous model manager, but I've never met him. Mace is such a liar. I can't trust anything he says. I try to dash past him, but he stops me with his strong hands on my upper arms. It stings like he's piercing my skin with needles.

"Whoa, turbo. You're not going anywhere."

I try to get my arm up near his face so I can throat punch him, but he's holding me in the iron-clad grips of his massive hands.

"Let me go!"

He wraps his trunk-like arms around my chest and pulls my back to his front. Tiny sparks explode from my skin like I've walked through a windstorm and slid down a metal slide. If I wasn't so weak I could think of a way to disable him, but I'm a mess right now. My arms and legs aren't listening to my brain. The heat from his body penetrates my skin, and I realize I'm wearing a hospital gown with the back open. No underwear. My naked butt is hanging out and scratching against the rough denim of his jeans.

He leans down and his deep voice vibrates in my ear. "Chill."

Gah! I hate him and his bossy voice. He's in total control over this situation, and I'm at his mercy. I want to fly through the roof to get away from him.

"You're still amped up."

"Amped up from what?"

Two nurses come in and pause when they see us in a clinch. He releases me, and I rush over to them. The IV cord pulls out and blood splashes onto the floor. "Oh my God. I'm bleeding."

MEMORIZING MACE

I can't stop staring at the bright red plasma pumping from my arm. I know blood is red, and I've bled before, but it's never been as vivid as this. Mace turns away and pulls his hair back as the nurses snap into action to reinsert the tube.

They guide me back to the bed and reattach the IV. "How are you feeling?" One of them talks to me while the other finishes cleaning up the blood.

"My arms and back are stinging. I have a headache. My hands won't stop shaking."

"Withdrawals. Drug overdose," Mace says in an accusatory tone.

"I don't do drugs. You're lying. He's a liar." I point at him and talk to the nurses like they are police officers.

"Do you want us to ask him to leave?" The nurse glances from me to him. She doesn't seem to be concerned with his presence and continues working on my arm. That's probably because he's so handsome no sane woman would throw him out of bed.

Mace stands silent in the corner, his face unreadable and brooding. Considering he's the only one who seems to know what's going on here, I probably shouldn't kick him out. "No." I hate it, but I need to deal with him.

"We'll send in your doctor." The nurses leave. I glare at Mace and cross my arms over my chest.

"Don't mess up the tubes again," he says as he folds down into his seat.

"Don't tell me what to do. Tell me what's happening." I'm not interested in sparring with him. I just need to know what's going on, so I can get out of here.

"I told you. I found you unconscious in a room on Arthur Morganna's island. There were needles on the bed. We brought you here to save your life." He sounds indignant like it's my fault he had to rescue me.

"Huh." This whole story is not adding up. I didn't do drugs, and I wasn't on any island.

"What the hell were you doing there?" He goes into accusation mode like I'm a murder suspect.

My mouth opens but nothing comes out. I shouldn't have to defend myself right now. I need answers from him. "What were *you* doing on the island?" I don't even know what he's talking about, but I'm gonna fake it till I make it.

"Did Giselle bring you there or did you go yourself?" He fires off another accusatory question.

"I don't know."

"You're lying."

Gah! I don't know anyone named Giselle. I've never met Arthur Morganna. I can't process this all right now. My hands fly up to my hair. "This is all so weird. I can't handle it."

A woman wearing a doctor's coat walks in looking concerned at first as she sees us having a heated argument. Then she smiles at me nicely. "I'm Dr. Darby. I specialize in opiate and narcotic addiction. I'm glad to see you awake and alert. They gave you an anti-overdose medication in the helicopter, and it probably saved your life." There was a helicopter too? I don't remember that either. Dr. Darby has a calm demeanor and seems very professional. I'm glad she's here. Finally someone I can trust.

"What kind of overdose?" I ask.

"We detected trace levels of heroin in your system."

"Heroin? I swear I don't do drugs. I don't even drink."

"It's possible then that it was against your will," Dr. Darby says quietly.

"Oh." I turn my questioning gaze toward Mace. "Who would do that to me?"

He holds up his hands. "Hey, now. No. It wasn't me. There were lots of people who saw me carry you out. I can't believe you're not being straightforward on this. It's too important to mess up."

I shake my head and stare at Dr. Darby, pleading with her to believe me and help me. "I'm being honest. I don't know Arthur Morganna or this Giselle person he's asking me about."

Mace huffs and shakes his head. "There was nobody else there. You had to have gone there with them. Even if they kidnapped you and drugged you, you should remember something."

Dr. Darby looks from Mace to me, assessing the situation with a calmness that seems beyond her years. "Do you remember anything about being kidnapped or drugged?"

I could lie, but I don't have the energy right now. "No. Nothing." There's a white space in my brain where I feel like I should have something, but it's empty.

"Do you know what day it is?" She starts scribbling notes on her clipboard.

What day is it? I don't know. "October something?" This is so frustrating.

"It's November fifteenth." Dr. Darby finishes her notes and places a comforting hand on my arm. "I'll call our brain injury specialist in to talk to you. He might order an MRI and some other tests, but it sounds like you're experiencing some memory loss induced by the drugs. It's not that uncommon."

Memory loss? "Like amnesia?"

"It appears so right now. We'll know more after your tests and meetings with the specialist."

I try again to access the part of my brain where yesterday should be, and it's just not there. It's scary, but it's an empty void. My body shows signs that match what Mace and Dr. Darby are saying. Could it be true? "If I did lose my memory, do you think it's permanent?" I whisper.

Mace has grown extremely quiet over in his corner. His foot is tapping, and his head is down again, staring at the floor. All the turbulence that was coming off him has shrunk away.

"I'm not sure, but there are some very talented doctors at this hospital that will help you. You're not alone. I'll go order the tests and check in on you later. You're doing fairly well otherwise, so that's good news, but please rest for at least a week until the drugs are out of your system."

I glare up at Dr. Darby. "If you knew me, you'd understand there is zero chance I'll rest for a week. That's not who I am."

She turns to Mace. "Even though she has no history of drug use, she still has a high risk of seeking out drugs and repeating the behavior so watch over her twenty-four-seven. Especially if the memories come back, she shouldn't be alone."

His head pops up. "I wasn't... I'm not..." Mace stutters and holds up his palms like he's warding off an evil spirit.

Dr. Darby's mouth curls up into a polite smile, but I can see in her eyes, she's not impressed with Mace at all. Neither am I right now. He's acting like a jerk, making a difficult situation even harder. "Do you have someone else you can call to stay with you?"

I shake my head, but it hurts, so I stop. "Listen. I really don't need a babysitter. I feel fine, and I will never do heroin. Trust me." If she knew me, she'd know how true that statement is. "I'd prefer to be alone while I wait for my memory to return."

"It's not a good idea for you to be alone. The memories could be quite traumatic. If you don't have someone, we can look into getting a nurse to stay with you." She gives Mace a castigating side-eye for not stepping up and offering to stay with me.

It's fine with me. The last thing I want is Mace Twist with me twenty-four-seven while I struggle to understand all that's happened.

Mace stands up and steps closer with his stern brow and hard eyes staring down at me. "You need to call someone to come look after you."

Our gazes meet close up for the first time. His eyes are a marbled cloud of sky blue, gray, and dark blue, really stunning against his darker skin. He's also inhumanly tall, and his head almost reaches the ceiling of the room. It all overwhelms me, and I blurt out the truth.

"I don't have anyone. All right?"

He freezes and narrows his brow so tight, deep furrows form on his forehead. He's scrutinizing me. The heat of his stare makes me uncomfortable, but I meet his gaze and hold it.

I shouldn't have said that. I revealed a weakness to him, and he'll use it against me the first chance he gets. I'm not on my game right now.

Mace and I continue our staring competition as Dr. Darby folds her clipboard under her arm and repeats a lot of the information she already said as if I may have forgotten it.

I haven't. In fact, my mind is already looking for the gaps. It's November and I don't remember anything since October. An entire month is lost deep in my brain. Sometime during that month, I got tied up in a convoluted mess with the Twist brothers.

After Dr. Darby leaves, I plop back with my head on the stiff hospital pillow and growl in frustration. "This sucks!"

"It's not so bad, Loralei. You're still alive. Thanks to me, I might add, and I didn't hear you offer any gratitude."

"You have no idea what this means for me. I could lose the most important part of my life. My job." I was so close to breaking my top case.

"What do you do?" The hard wrinkles are back on his brow.

"I'm a cop! I can't have heroin in my system. Doesn't matter how it got there. I could get fired."

His jaw tightens, and he runs a hand through his hair quickly, twice. "You're a cop?" Apparently, I've blown his mind. Is it so hard to believe I'm in law enforcement? I'm weak right now, but I'm a formidable cop when I'm at my best.

"Do you have a problem with that?" He's a bounty hunter. He works with cops all the time. If he's following the law, he shouldn't have any issues with my job.

His gaze darts to the curtain at the exit, then back to his chair, and to me again. Without a word or a look back, he starts to walk out of the room.

"Are you leaving?" If he leaves, I'm stuck in this situation all alone. I don't have my purse, my clothes, no ID or cash. I'd rather have my worst enemy here than be alone right now.

"I don't know," he says quietly as he passes through the curtain door.

Unfortunately, I know from painful experience Mace is the kind of guy who would walk out on a girl in dire straits like me. That's what he does. He walks in, makes a mess, and leaves others behind to deal with the cleanup.

Well, guess what I do? I take care of things myself. If I need something, I go get it. I don't sit helpless and dependent on men like Mace. I've been alone since I was eighteen, and this is just another stumbling block. I'll figure out a way forward.

First though, I need this headache to go away, so I close my eyes and try to forget Mace was ever here. Within a minute, I give up on that. There's no denying he was here. He filled the room, he rattled me with his intensity and good looks, and I will never ever forget the sight of Mace's backside walking out on me today.

Chapter 3 Negotiations

Mace

"She could lose her job, she can't remember getting kidnapped, she has no one to come pick her up, the doctor said she has a high risk of seeking out heroin again..." Cutter listens quietly on the phone as I'm sitting in my truck in the hospital parking lot.

"And?" Cutter has no sympathy for Loralei after the pain she's caused us, but he didn't see the lost-child look in the eyes of a woman who is usually well put together and confident. He also didn't see how beautiful she is now.

"I'm feeling obligated to help her," I admit.

"You're not." Cutter doesn't even think about it. He wants nothing to do with her, and I don't blame him.

She's been raining down random acts of revenge on me and my family for six years. She's never forgiven me for using her to bring in her fallen-from-grace father. I was just doing my job, but she's never gotten over it.

Now I'm torn between helping her or bailing on this whole situation. "I'm also feeling a rope being tied round my wrists, and I'm wanting to cut and run."

"Cut and run then. She's on her own." Cutter makes it seem so simple. Why can't I just do it?

"I thought you wanted Loralei to help us with Giselle." He asked me that just a few hours ago.

"Not worth getting mixed up with her."

I grunt in agreement.

"Mace?"

"Huh?"

"Cut and run. You're not obligated."

"Mm-hmm."

"Holy shit. You want to fuck her. Don't you?"

My grunt is non-committal this time. I want to fuck her, no doubt. I want other things too that I'm not willing to think about right now. I've always been tempted to go after her again. I held back because I assumed she was happy, didn't need my shit in her life. Now I know for a fact she has no one. Why? She doesn't have one person she can call from the hospital? I'm supposed to walk away from her when she's in a tough spot?

"No, Mace. Jeez." Cutter reads my silence over the line. "She's trouble."

"I'm not afraid of her." She's all of five-foot-seven with her petite little body. She's a cop though, so she has a gun and knows how to use it, which only makes me want her more.

"Plenty of other women out there who aren't psychos trying to exact revenge on you." I can almost hear him pacing the room back at home.

"Psycho chicks are wicked hot in bed." She was a live wire the first time at eighteen. I can only imagine how she's evolved as she became a grown woman.

"No, man. Get that thought out of your head. Cut and run." Cutter is speaking reason, but I don't want to hear it right now.

"Let me talk to Mom."

There's static on the phone as Cutter finds my mom and talks to her with a hushed voice. I hear him mention Loralei losing her job and "psycho" and "what to do" but luckily he leaves out anything sounding like "bang her" or "sex."

"Mace?" My mom sounds alarmed by whatever Cutter told her. "Should I come down and help her?"

"No. She's the one who brought your old family down on us." My mom's mafia-boss uncle from New York showed up at Twist Cabins a year after I was with Loralei. He told us she said he could find my mom in California with Foster Dunham, my dad's previous name. It all worked out, but it was a tense situation with my dad prepared to defend my mom again like he had to do before they were married.

"I know who she is and what she did. It doesn't matter. She's in a bad situation. We can't abandon her. I'll bring her some clothes and things."

That's my mom. Doesn't hold a grudge and would never consider bailing on her like I'm thinking of doing.

"Please don't come down here. I'll handle it."

She sighs. "All right," she says reluctantly. "I trust you'll do the right thing, Mace. You always do in the end." God, I don't deserve that woman for a mom. She has way too much faith in me.

"Thanks, Ma. I'll call you later."

I end the call and start up my truck. I know what I need to do.

***

Later that afternoon, I drop a handful of shopping bags on Loralei's hospital bed.

She sits up and stares at the pile. "What's this?"

"Clothes, shoes. Blue stripes and headbands. All that nautical stuff you like."

"Wow. Thank you." She digs into the bags and removes the tissue paper. "These are exactly my style."

"You can't walk out of here in a gown with your ass hanging out the back." As beautiful as it may be, she needs to cover it.

"I hadn't even thought about it. Today has been so busy with tests and phone calls." She wipes her forehead and takes a deep breath. She looks calmer now, more like her normal self.

"You ready to be discharged?"

"Yes." She exaggerates the word like she's dying to get out of here.

"I'll take you home."

She pauses and tilts her head. "Why? Why did you come back? I thought you'd left."

"I almost did. Then I realized that would be a dick thing to do, so here I am."

Her wide-eyed gaze travels from me to the bags. She doesn't look excited about leaving with me, but she doesn't have a lot of options. "Huh. Well, okay. Let me get dressed and signed out."

***

As she climbs into my old beat-up Chevy, her eyes scan over the cracked dashboard and mess of necklaces hanging from the rearview mirror. She frowns like she's just climbed into a porta-potty.

She grew up the daughter of a famous celebrity. He was all about self-actualization and living your best life. She's looking down on me and my beater truck. "It's not a Maserati, but it has character."

She peers over at me with wide eyes. "What? Oh no. It's not your truck. Just got a lot on my mind."

I start up the truck and head in the direction of her place in Sausalito. I shouldn't ask, but my curiosity keeps eating at me. "Like what?" She was so animated and feisty at the hospital. Now she's subdued. It's more than just the drugs wearing off. Something else is wrong with her.

"I talked to my supervisor. She put me on unpaid leave pending investigation." She looks down, obviously ashamed to tell me this, which she doesn't need to be.

"That seems harsh. It wasn't your fault."

"She kept saying they need to verify my story, as if she thinks I did drugs intentionally. I can't even prove I didn't."

The deep sorrow in her voice hits me in the gut. "She's not giving you any breaks?"

"Nope. I thought I had earned some respect from her with all the hard work I've been doing. I could even understand paid leave, but unpaid leave is a slap in the face."

My stomach roils at all the unfair hits this girl is taking. "Not cool. You're the victim here. They shouldn't be punishing you. That's why I could never be a cop."

She raises her head and narrows her eyes at me. "Tell me about Morganna. My supervisor said she couldn't discuss it with me."

Oh shit. I could lie to her, but she deserves the truth from someone right now. "Morganna is Cutter and Sutton's biological father, and he abused them as children before they ran away."

She gasps, and her fingers come up to her lips.

"It's a long story, but Morganna threatened Cutter's girl, Cass, and Cutter killed him. You were passed out while it happened. I found you after we arrived, and the authorities were on their way."

She nods slowly. It must be so hard for her to hear all this and not even remember any of it. "And Giselle?"

I take a deep breath and give her more truth. "Giselle worked with Morganna to lure Cass to the island."

Her hand tightens into a fist. "This could all tie into my case."

"What case?"

"My first undercover assignment. It was gonna make my career. It's all up in smoke now that I'm on leave. I can't touch it."

I'm curious, and Cutter wanted me to ask more about Giselle, but I don't want to get involved in her cases. She can't remember anything anyway. I'm just bringing her home, dropping her off, and making my getaway.

When we pull up in the drive of her place, there's a man peeking inside her front window.

Slamming the truck into park, I jump out and pounce on him from behind. He hits the bushes and groans.

"Mace! Stop!"

I push the guy's face into the geraniums. "He was breaking into your house."

"No. He wasn't. He was probably just looking for me. He's my ex."

I let the guy up, and he grimaces as he wipes the dirt off his slacks and dress shirt. He's a ruffled up pretty boy.

"Who the hell are you?" he asks me.

I don't answer him and look back at Loralei.

"You could've asked me before you tackled me." He has a derpy voice too.

"It looked shifty." I shrug.

We follow Loralei inside, and he walks straight to the kitchen sink, urgently scrubbing the tiny specks on his stupid shirt. What a douche nozzle. He didn't even try to fight back. She dated this guy?

The place is decorated like the inside of a ship. Portholes, anchor pillows, lots of rattan and navy stripes, potted palms. Neat and tidy like her clothes.

Her ex comes out of the kitchen with a big wet stain on his shirt. He's tall and skinny. Dweeb factor ten. He's the guy that sits at the front of the class nodding and smiling and taking detailed notes just to impress the teacher, but he's really dumb and fails the class anyway.

"Mace, this is Griffin." Loralei motions between us with an awkward smile.

I tilt my chin, but I don't give a shit what his name is. I'm already turning around and heading for the door.

"Mace! Wait!" She shuffles up behind me. "I wanted to thank you."

"No problem." I take the stairs of her porch two at a time. I'm almost free. I can feel the ropes around my wrists going slack as the fresh air hits my face.

"I was hoping you'd stay for a minute."

"Nope." I keep walking to my truck, forcing her to run to keep up with me.

"I need to ask you something."

This feels like a trap. Anything this girl wants to ask me is laced with arsenic, and I'd be stupid to fall for it. "Ask Griffin. I'm out of here."

"Griffin can't help me. I need you."

The desperation in her voice slows me down. I need to stop falling for it, but it's compelling. I can't seem to say no to this girl when she begs. "What do you need me for?"

When I stop to look at her, I'm struck again by how pretty she is. Even with no makeup and her hair a mess, she's stunning.

"Can you help me remember?" She looks down like she's suddenly shy. "I hate having to ask you this, but I need my memories back. I want to know who did this so I can clear my name, and I want to keep working my active case. It could be related."

Huh. If she's on leave from work, she probably shouldn't be hunting down cases. "Bending the rules, are we?"

"Just this one case. It's too high-profile to give up on, and it'll help restore my credibility when I get back."

"And what makes you think I'm the man to do this?"

"I know you followed me."

That gets my attention. "How'd you know that?"

"I heard you tell Cutter over the phone."

All right. I thought she spotted me while I was tracking her. I'm an old pro. One of the best bounty hunters out there. No way she saw me. "I did track you because you showed up at my family's place, looking all innocent with your navy blue headband, but you were suspicious as hell. Reappearing in my life the same night a fight happened to break out? I had to see what you were up to."

"So you know where I went. Take me back there. Help trigger the memories. I know they're in there just below the surface." She steps closer, and the neediness in her big brown eyes is incredibly tempting again. This girl is a cop, and she hates me. It must be so hard for her to lower herself to my level and ask for help.

Back on her porch, Griffin is standing inside the open doorway looking on with curiosity, but I don't think he can hear us. I keep my voice down just in case.

"No." It's hard to say to her, but I seriously need to make my escape and get back to work.

"Please."

God. Her begging reaches down to my dick and squeezes. "No. I did the right thing. I got you home safe. Now I check out and hit the road."

She sets her brow, ready to battle. Cute. "What can I offer you to make you say yes?"

"Oh you want to negotiate? Okay. How about you let me park my truck in your garage of love?"

She stares at me blankly, her mouth opening slightly. "Park your truck in my... Eww. No." Her head flinches back and her brows smash together. "I'd rather bathe in Brussels sprouts than see you naked."

"Really? You don't like Brussels sprouts?"

"They are the seed of Satan."

"No they're not." They aren't my favorite, but they aren't the worst veggie out there. "Cauliflower is much worse than Brussels sprouts."

She shakes her head. "Your vegetable preferences don't matter. Dr. Darby suggested revisiting the places where the memories first occurred."

"Revisiting?"

"Yes. Here's my offer. You take me to all the places you saw me go, and I'll forgive you." She crosses her arms over her chest like she's a genie in a bottle who has granted me three wishes.

"You'll forgive me?"

Griffin walks down the steps toward us, and I tilt my head to alert Loralei to keep it quiet.

"Something wrong?" he asks in his nasally twang. Dweeb.

"No. Just go, Griffin. Thanks for checking on me, but I'm fine really."

He gives me the once over, trying to look cool. "Okay. You call me if you need me."

"Sure." Her tone says she's placating him. She'll never call him. Now me, she said she "needs."

Griffin walks to a black Lexus and glares at us as he takes off, and I can't help but smirk at her and her lameass ex.

"Let's go back inside and talk." She walks away, and I'm looking at her ass, which is nice and round, just like I like 'em.

Talking is worse than cauliflower to me, but negotiating with her is intriguing, so I take the bait and follow her.

Back inside, she pulls out a wooden chair for me at her kitchen table. "Would you like something to drink?"

"Just talk." I take the seat and lean back.

"Okay." She counts on her fingers. "I estimate I've forgotten the time period between October ninth and November fifteenth which overlaps with the time that you followed me."

"That seems... accurate." I thought memory loss would be less specific, but she's the type to keep track of it to the day. "I only followed you for a couple days after the fight. The rest of the time, you're on your own."

She takes that in and frowns then seems to talk herself out of it. "That's okay. I'll take any info you have. So here's the deal. You take me back to all the places I visited, and I'll forgive you for what you did to my dad."

I stare at her for a long time trying to process her schtick here. "Your dad did that to himself by skipping bail on drug charges and not paying his child support."

She growls and turns to the fridge. She comes back with a bottle of water and slaps it down on the table. "He shouldn't have had to die over some missed payments."

I take the bottle and slowly twist open the cap. "He didn't die because of me. Is that what you think?" She's more unhinged than I thought.

"*You* put him in prison." She seriously blames me for her dad being a drug-addicted loser?

"He had warrants. I delivered him. The shit that went down after that was out of my hands." I thought this was obvious.

"He wouldn't have even been in prison if it weren't for you, and he wouldn't have killed himself."

"That's a stretch there, Lola." I'm not even sure if the guy killed himself. There's rumors he was taken out.

She freezes and stares at me. "My dad called me Lola."

"Then I'll stop." I take a sip of water.

"No. It's fine."

"So, say I take you on the Lola Bay Area Tour, and you forgive me, you leave me and my family alone forever?" Her plan sounds ridiculous to me, but also tempting. It would give me more opportunities to mess with her head and something to hold over her if she continues to show up at Twist Cabins.

"Yes." She smiles like she thinks she's making progress.

"And what if I don't forgive you?"

Her brow draws together. "Forgive me for what?"

I don't buy her innocent act for a second. "Don't play me, girl. Let's start with the retaliation for hauling in your dad."

Her lips sputter, and her eyes glow with mischief. "You didn't like the glitter dildos on your truck?"

"No."

She laughs. "What about the plastic wrap? I thought that added a nice touch."

"I let you have that because it did look like I duped you to get to him. I understand why you were angry."

"You didn't just dupe me. You took my virginity and then arrested my father before I was even dressed!"

"I don't see it that way." I take a sip of water and watch her eyes move to my throat as I swallow it.

She makes a gulping sound, and then shakes her head. "How do you see it?"

"I admit I did come to the party to find out more about your father. Once I saw you, I wasn't thinking about him at all. I was thinking you were the prettiest girl I'd ever seen."

Her breath hitches. "You were?"

My nod and wink causes her to turn away stiffly. She paces to the fridge and comes back with another water bottle. She's cute when she's flustered. "We talked. I knew before you told me you were a virgin. There was this untarnished pureness about you." I remember her big doe eyes, shiny hair, and painted nails. Her dad took care of her like a rare jewel. She was sheltered from all the ugliness of life. Traveling with him on his road show of positivity.

"So you decided to take it?" The water bottle crinkles and deforms under the pressure of her clenching fist.

She's trying to goad me into fighting with her, but I'm not falling for it. I know the best way to diffuse this. "Let's say you were color-blind your entire life, and all you ever wanted was to see blue with your own eyes. You'd heard of blue. People had told you blue was beautiful like the sky, but you'd never seen it yourself. What if someone offered you a chance not only to see blue but touch it? The catch is you'd only have one precious moment to hold the sky. Would you do it?"

She stares over my head, her eyes unfocused, her lower lip falling slightly. "I would," she whispers.

"So would I. Blue was as impressive as I always thought it would be. I held the sky in my hands for a moment that flew by too fast, but don't think I didn't treasure it and understand the magnitude of it." I clear my throat. "Then I went back to my black and white life. I had a job to do. I brought your dad in. End of story." I shrug and take a sip of water. I didn't intend to share that much detail with her, but now it's out there.

Her lips slowly close and flatten into a firm line as the fire returns to her eyes. "It wasn't the end of the story for me. My dad went to prison. He killed himself. He was in debt. I had to unenroll from Stanford and start working. I fought like a dog and clawed my way back to earn everything I have now." She motions around her place, but it's mostly empty apart from her maritime decor.

"I don't see how any of that is my fault." I screw the cap back on the water bottle.

"Of course you don't." She sits opposite me and roughly jerks her water bottle open.

"No matter what I did, you crossed the line later when you broadcast my parents' location."

"I didn't do that."

"I have proof you did it. My family is still sour on you for that." My mom could've been killed because of her stupid vendetta. "Then years later, you come up to my parents' place and gossip with the neighbors? Why? You can't let it go? You holding on so hard to vengeance?"

"I didn't know it would blow up into a huge fight." She shakes her head.

"Yes you did. You're not stupid. You calculated the whole thing. I asked around. I know you told Jareth that Cutter pulled a knife on Pepper. You set off a chain of events that caused a huge group of bikers to come up to Twist Cabins and challenge us. We were outnumbered. I saw you sneak out after the fight."

"I can't believe you recognized me after all these years."

"I'd recognize you for the rest of my life." My voice softens.

She leans in closer. "Really?"

I bend forward too, so she can see the honesty in my eyes. "On the helicopter, I knew it was you as soon as I got the hair out of your face."

"Wow."

I'm telling her too much. Everything I reveal is a vulnerability she can use against me later. "Don't be flattered. It's because you're a threat to my family. I protect my own."

She stays quiet because she knows she's in the wrong, and we've reached the end of this conversation.

"Anyway. I don't see anything in this for me. You forgive me, but I still hate you." I stand up and walk toward the door. I need to get back to work and get out of this nightmare.

She follows me. "Fine. What do you want in return?"

I smirk and peruse her tits. They are quite nice, pert and round. I've been alone in the Mojave for a month, and I'm parched.

"No way. No parking your truck in my garage of love." She crosses her arms over her chest.

I lean down and speak quietly in her ear. "Just imagine. It could be like the first time. You moaning my name, riding me like a cowgirl, sucking every inch of my body like I'm cotton candy."

She gasps and pulls away. "You remember that?"

"I've got it memorized." I tap my temple. One of the best nights of my life.

"It wasn't that great. You're a figment of your own imagination."

"Sure." I scoff at her futile lies.

She looks like she's about to say something, but she snaps out of it. "I'm not sleeping with you, Mace. You take me where I need to go, I forgive you. That'll be huge for me because I've hated you for a long freaking time. I don't give a frick if you forgive me or not, but I won't retaliate anymore. That's my proposal. Take it or leave it."

You have to admire her spunk. She's the one who needs something from me, and she's acting like she has the upper hand.

I plop down on her anchor couch and make a point of loudly smacking my boots on her glass coffee table. "Deal. Do you need to rest first?"

She sputters like she's surprised I agreed to her stupid plan. "No. I'm fine."

"Then go get ready." This is probably a very bad idea, but I'm enjoying teasing her, and I like the challenge of getting her in bed again. She should know better than to dare me.

"Where are we going?"

"We're going to a nightclub. Dress appropriately." I pull out my phone and wave her off with my hand. She's fun to mess with, but I'm done with all this talking.

She growls and stomps into her bedroom.

I've got her off her game, and I'm enjoying it.

I dial up Helix, my fellow bounty hunter.

If I'm gonna recreate that night at Dragon Lounge, I'm gonna need him to do me some favors. I'll owe him again after this, but it'll be so worth it to watch Loralei react.

Chapter 4 Dragon Lounge

Loralei

Two hours later, I emerge from my bedroom and find Mace still sitting on my couch with his feet still on the coffee table.

The clearing of my throat causes him to snap up and rise to his towering six-foot-seven height.

Holy crap. He's changed his clothes too. He must have had them in his truck. Camel-colored suede pants wrap around his trunk-like thighs and flare out at the bottom above chocolate cowboy boots. Fringe from a matching suede jacket dangles from silver star buckles. Several layers of jade and crystal pendant necklaces hang on jute strings around his neck. Hair loose and skull rings on display, he seems like he's just returned from an adventure at a bohemian cowboy tower of doom and yet he looks delicious. Somehow he pulls it all off. The man is a walking house of style and, unlike me, it's effortless.

His gaze traverses my all-black ensemble of pencil skirt, blouse, and pointy heels.

He shakes his head. "Try again. Think inner lioness."

"What do you mean?"

"You're stepping over to the dark side to interrogate criminals wanted for... What's your case about?"

I intentionally didn't tell him. He finally asked. "It's a missing person."

His eyebrows arch, and he purses his lips like he's impressed. What did he think it was, shoplifting? I wouldn't break all the rules and keep pursuing this case if it wasn't something big.

"Male or female?"

"Female."

He nods and turns back to the couch. His outfit is even more spectacular from the backside. "Wear what you wore last time."

"What did I wear?" I hate having to ask Mace questions like this. I should know exactly what I wore because I would've picked it out carefully.

"A slinky leopard strappy thing with fuchsia lace." He motions toward me from head to toe.

Wow. For someone who hates me, Mace is freakishly observant of my clothes and remembers details of what I wore.

"That's my nightie!"

He shrugs. "Whatever it takes, right? And change your shoes too. They had a thicker, higher heel, and the toes weren't so witch-like."

"These are not witch-like, but okay. I have other shoes."

He plops back on the couch and crosses his long legs at the ankle, huge boots sticking up into the air. "I bet you do."

What does he mean by that?

***

I can't believe I'm about to walk out into my living room and stand in front of Mace Twist in a nightie and leopard heels. I bought these for a Halloween costume when I was younger and they are incredibly uncomfortable, but the heel is high and the front is a rounded wedge. Definitely more lioness and less witch-like.

Shoulders back, head high, here we go. Mace turns and stands slowly with his gaze glued to my dress.

"Better?"

His attention sweeps over my breasts—which I spent extra time pushing up while ensuring proper nipple coverage—then stops on my shoes.

A warm glow simmers in his eyes, and his lips curl up slowly. "Rawr. That's it. Inner lioness has come out to play." His raspy voice giving me a vivid compliment makes my tummy twirl, but I can't let it get to me. Yes, I look good. He's a man. It's normal for him to react. I'm dressed for the part. So is he.

"Shall we go?" This mutual inspection has lasted long enough. Let's get some work done.

"Give me the keys to your Maserati." He holds out his hand, palm up.

"Uh, no."

"I'll drive."

"No. Not my baby." I worked my butt off to buy that car. Not giving Mace Twist the keys. Nope.

"It won't get a scratch. You can't drive in those shoes anyway."

"I'll take them off."

"We're gonna roll up at the Dragon Lounge, and you're gonna get out barefoot and put your shoes on? Might as well wear your badge and carry a red siren over your head. Give me the keys." He steps closer and I step back.

Should I give him a shot? Maybe this would be a good chance to see if I can trust him. "Fine. I actually lost my keys. Let me get the spare."

I feel his eyes on my back as I pull the spare keys out of my office desk. "Don't go over the speed limit or get pulled over. I don't want anyone from work to see me like this."

He nods and bends at the waist in a bow as he accepts them from me. "Of course."

We walk to the inner garage door, and I click the opener.

A loud pop blasts in the corner by the outer garage door.

Mace tackles me and we topple over. My elbow hits the floor hard, and his weight presses me to the tile. "Get off me."

The scent of burned carbon wafts in through the door. He closes it with his foot. "You all right?"

"Yes. Get off me so we can go see what it was."

"You stay here." He climbs up and reaches for the door.

"No. Something just exploded in my garage. I'm not staying here."

He opens the door slowly and peeks around. The smoke has cleared, and there's no one in the street. We run out to the sidewalk, but no one is around.

"What the hell was that? You storing something in your garage that might explode?"

"No. It seemed like it was outside the door. It was like a firework or something."

"That was bigger than a firework." He inspects the dust and debris near the corner.

"We're not calling the cops." I don't want any more attention drawn to me.

He looks up at me and smirks. "I wasn't gonna call the cops."

"Good."

He laughs. I know it's odd for a cop not to call the cops, but I'm on leave and going rogue here. I don't want an even bigger investigation into me.

He stands up and brushes the ash off his hands. "We still going to the club?"

"Sure. Not gonna let a little firework stop me."

"Get in the car. We'll talk more on the way. Hold up." He drops to his stomach and looks under the car. He checks the bumper and the tires. I can't lay down in this dress, but I check the interior through the windows.

"It looks clear." He clicks the doors open, and we both get in. We stare at each other and catch our breath. "That was unexpected," I say.

He's quiet as he starts up the car, but his brow is furrowed and his shoulders stiff. As we pull out into the street, he asks, "Did you tell anyone else you were home except Griffin?"

"You think Griffin did that? It could've been set before I was kidnapped."

"True. This means someone is on to you. Possibly the person who kidnapped you or the people who have your missing person."

"Or they are one in the same."

"Could be."

"Someone wants me to stop investigating this case. You see why I can't stop?"

He nods. "This shit just got interesting."

***

We arrive at Dragon Lounge, and Mace was right. It would've been suspicious if I drove considering the outfits we're wearing.

He waves off the valet and parks himself.

"What's our plan?" I ask him.

"No plan."

"No plan?"

"Plans screw things up. Prepare for the unexpected."

That's the opposite of everything we learn at the academy, but he's all I've got right now. "I don't even know who I'm looking for."

"If he's here, I'll give you the signal."

"What's the signal?"

He shrugs. "You'll know when I give it to you."

"I'm not liking this." I grumble under my breath and get out of the car.

He comes around and puts a hand on my back which makes me shiver and tense. See? This is why we need a plan because I wouldn't have agreed to pretending to be with him, but it's too late. The valets have eyes on us, and there's a huge crowd. I tighten up my body and do my best to impersonate a girl who would be happy to be at a club with a giant rhinestone cowboy.

Mace attracts a ton of attention as he struts up to the entrance. From the looks on the female's faces, they'd be thrilled to walk up here with Mace at their side, but they don't know him and the evils he's capable of.

Mace works out a deal with the doorman, and we pass through the red velvet rope ahead of the line.

"How'd you do that?"

"I have connections."

With his hand on my back again, we make our way through the rows of high-backed booths. Illuminated dragons glow on the walls, and young people dressed in sleek clothes pack in around the bar and dance floor. The loud bass of the hip hop beat pounds in my ears. It's so loud, fighting it is futile. You have no choice but to let it vibrate through your entire body.

Mace must feel it too because he grabs my hand and smiles as he leads me to the bar. "What do you drink?"

"I don't drink."

He shakes his head and rolls his eyes. His hand grips mine tighter as he leans in to get the bartender's attention. He towers over everyone and the bartender is female, so he gets served right away.

As we're waiting for our drinks, I scan the room for anyone familiar. None of this feels like I've seen it before. Not even a little déjà vu. Mace could be making this whole thing up, and I wouldn't know. Depending on him makes me nervous.

His possessive hold on my hand, the energy in the club, the way we're dressed, it's all getting to me, and I'm trying hard to remember this is for work because if it wasn't, I'd be enjoying it far too much.

The bartender passes him two drinks, and he finally lets go of my hand to juggle the drinks and his wallet. His drink is a short, cylindrical glass with dark brown liquid in it. No ice. Mine is a vibrant yellow color in a similar glass, but it has a cherry and ice.

"What's this?" I ask as he hands it to me.

"Whiskey sour. Try it." I take the glass from him and he raises his over our heads. "To my arch-enemy, for having fuck-me shoes in her closet ready to go."

It's loud in here, and I'm not sure I heard him right, but oh my word, Mace saying *fuck-me* in my ear has to be one of the most erotic things I've ever experienced, apart from actually sleeping with him, which is still at the top of that list.

He leans back and takes a sip from his drink. My eyes are glued to his mouth as he swirls it around and his Adam's apple when he swallows. Everything he does is so blatantly sexual, it should be illegal.

I take a small sip of my drink, and the tart lemon takes the bitter edge off the whiskey. "Not bad."

Leaning back with his elbows on the bar, he scans the room. I still don't see anyone I recognize. This entire exercise is a massive waste of time and energy. "I don't think this is working."

He ignores me like he can't hear me over the music, which he probably can't. "We need to draw some attention to ourselves," he says while staring out over my head.

"What? No!" But I'm too late, he's already dragging me out to the dance floor. My drink splashes as I reach to set it down on the bar.

He pulls me through the crowd and stops dead center in the middle. I'm afraid of what he'll do next, but I'm stuck out here with him. A new song comes on and a wicked grin blooms on his face like they're playing it just for him. It's a grungy rock song, and his hips start moving to the vicious beat.

"C'mon. Dance, Lola."

His whole body is vibrating to the music now, and the heat coming off of him is making me sweat. I start to move to the music but only a little, shifting my weight from foot to foot.

"Put your hips into it." He makes a circle with his hips.

My cheeks are flaming hot. I never draw attention to myself like this, and Mace is far too comfortable with it.

His hands grab my hips and sway them back and forth. "Think inner lioness." He makes a rawr sound and a tiger claw with his hand. He's ridiculous and also gorgeous. It's very hard to resist him. This is for a job after all. I let my hips go loose and finally start feeling the beat.

"That's it. Woot!"

He takes off his jacket and tosses it into the crowd.

Oh my God, he's crazy.

The chorus of the song says "*Porn Star Dancing,*" and I have to laugh at Mace for picking the perfect song to start stripping in a club. He goes for the buttons of his shirt, and I reach out to stop him.

"Mace, no."

"Why not?" His hands are stronger than mine, and he has his shirt open in seconds. He's pulling it over his shoulders, and I'm flashed with his massive hairy chest, ripped abs, and tattoos. He's a feast for the eyes. Several people have started to watch him now that he's half naked.

And oh my, with his shirt and jacket off, his pants are more visible. I'm trying not to stare, but I think he's half-hard, and I can see the outline of a giant penis in his pants.

He's not self-conscious at all. In fact, I bet he's proud of his penis imprint on his suede pants.

I have to laugh at the ridiculousness of it all. The laughter breaks through my inhibitions, and I find myself dancing with him too. My arms go up, and my hips sway. It's fun and sexy and so different from my normal life. Time to let go and be grateful I'm alive.

He pulls me close with a paw around the small of my back. I'm pressed up against his bare chest, and my hands come up to brace myself. He bends us left and right in some kind of banana move that is both sexy and stupid. A thin sheen of sweat makes his skin damp and shiny.

Finally the song ends, and he's beaming with pride as he walks us back to our seats. About ten girls immediately bound up to him and push me out of the way.

Someone else's arm circles around my waist and pulls me back. I turn, ready to fight.

"Hey, Loralei." A man with a mostly shaved, tattooed head is smiling down at me.

I look back at Mace for some kind of sign. He stands up and points. "That's him." He mouths it, but I get what he's saying. Pretty much everyone in the bar gets it.

"Uh, hey."

"You need some more favors from old Helix here?"

Helix. His name is Helix. It fits with the biometric tattoos all over his body including his scalp. He looks more like a machine than a human.

"Actually I need the same favors again." I have to arch my neck and pull him down to get his ear. "Can we go somewhere and talk?"

"Without doubt." He grabs my hand and walks me toward the back of the club.

Mace stays behind with his gaggle of girls. A tickle of apprehension grips my throat, but I push it down. I'm a cop. I can handle being alone with this guy even if he is tall and scary and I'm unarmed. No place to hide a gun with this outfit.

He takes me out to a small balcony with a loveseat and pulls my hand until I'm sitting next to him. The cool evening air raises goosebumps on my skin as he puts his arm behind me over the back of the seat. The music is muted out here, so I don't have to scream at him to be heard. "So, those favors?"

His head tilts to the side as he examines me. "What do you mean?"

"Can you do the same favors again for me?"

He scratches his shaved head and chuckles without smiling. "You didn't hear Morganna's dead?"

"Oh, yeah, I did hear that. I mean the other favor." Please let there have been more than one favor.

"You didn't get what you needed from Marval last time?"

Okay. This is good. Marval. I don't know anyone named Marval. "No, I didn't. Can you set it up again?"

"You want to take another shot at Marval Diablo Rios?"

Excellent. Now I have a name. Diablo does not sound good. "Yes."

He shakes his head and tsk-tsks me. "This is not wise. Why don't you come sit on my lap for a minute, and we'll talk about it up close and personal?"

I don't know what I told him about why I wanted Marval, but I need him to remind me, so I'm going to have to give in on this one.

With a coy smile, I make a move to climb up onto his thick thighs as strong hands grip my hips and pull my knees on either side of him. The heat from his body immediately hits me. I didn't realize before, but Helix has stunning silver eyes. He's actually a good looking guy underneath his harsh external appearance, and his shoulders feel sturdy when I brace my hands on them.

"Is this about your old man?"

I blink several times and stare at him in shock. My dad had something to do with Marval Diablo Rios? "Why would it be about my dad?"

He shrugs. "Thought you might be digging into the past."

I may have lost my memory, but I know I wasn't looking into my dad's associates. "No. I just want to talk with him." I twirl my fingertip around his ear. These tattoos are actually really well done. The dark and light are drawn in a way that it appears three dimensional like someone has actually cut his scalp away to reveal metal gears and thick bolts. "So you'll set me up with him?" I adjust myself on his lap, and he looks down at where my dress has slid up.

His tongue juts out and swipes his lower lip. "I'll see what I can do."

"Thank you." I embrace him with a hug and he stiffens. His hands come off my hips, and he holds them up in the air.

When I pull back, he's staring over my shoulder, his face drawn. Behind me, Mace stands in the entrance to the balcony. He has one foot kicked out and all his weight on one hip. His mouth hangs slightly open, and his eyes look sharp as razors. He's wearing his jacket without the shirt underneath, and he looks incredibly hot.

Helix's hands return to my hips but only to lift me up and plant me next to him on the seat. Helix stands up and wipes his hands together. "I'll get back to you on that, Loralei."

Mace glares at Helix as he leaves the balcony. I stand up and face down Mace. "I was making progress with him."

"You didn't have to sit on his face to get what you needed." He leans down and forces me to step backward.

"Why do you care what I do?"

My back hits the plexiglass wall around the balcony.

"Do you know who he is? He's a bounty hunter, yes, but he's also a hitman. A trained assassin. And you crawled up on his lap like he's a stripper. You were probably sitting on at least three loaded guns." He has me pinned with his hips, his hands above us on the plexiglass, and I am face to face with the gorgeous hair on his naked chest.

"Who was acting like a stripper tonight? You literally took off your clothes! The girls were all over you." I have to close my eyes to stop all the sensations he's throwing at me. He's too beautiful, too hot, too close.

He grins. "That was fun." And his smile is dazzling.

I push against his chest but he won't budge. "We're not here for fun!"

"I am always up for fun, no matter the job. You take it where you can get it. You should try it sometime."

"What's that supposed to mean?"

He looks over my head, out at the view of the city. "Never mind." He pushes off the wall, and his smile fades into a grimace. He takes my hand and pulls me back into the club. He waves goodbye to Helix and walks us back down to my car.

I'm scuffling along in my ridiculous leopard heels behind him trying to keep up. "You know him?"

He shrugs. "Bounty hunters stick together."

I stop to take off my shoes. "Did you tell him I'd be there tonight?"

"I may have mentioned it."

"Did he know about my missing memories?" I'm standing on the cold asphalt in bare feet, but it feels so good to be free.

He leans down and grabs my upper arm. "Hop on. I'll carry you."

"No. This dress."

"Hop on!" He tugs me up and over like he's putting on a jacket, and somehow I'm getting a piggyback ride down to my car in the parking lot. I find myself smiling. When was the last time I rode on a giant's back? Probably not since I was a kid and my dad carried me like this.

"I wouldn't tell Helix you lost your memory because it would put you at risk if he was the kidnapper. I protected you. From the looks of it, it's not him, so we're good."

"I agree. I don't think it's him. He said he'll hook me up with someone named Marval Diablo Rios."

He stops cold, ten feet away from the car. "Do you know who he is?"

"No."

He glances back over his shoulder at me. "He's a Venezuelan cartel boss."

Oh good Lord. I had a meeting with a cartel boss, and I don't remember? "Did you know I met with him before?"

"No." He starts walking again and finally stops at the passenger door to my Maserati before dropping me to my feet. "That's where I blew it. I stopped following you too soon. Nothing you were doing looked like it was related to me or my family, so I took off. Was chasing a skip in Arizona when I got the call." He looks down and shuffles his feet.

"It's okay, Mace. It's not your fault. You couldn't have known I was headed for trouble."

He shakes his head. "If I had just stuck with you a little longer, I might have been able to stop it."

"You don't know that."

He looks at me and nods, but I don't think I've convinced him. He feels a sense of guilt for my kidnapping, and I don't know what really happened. As far as I can tell, it had nothing to do with him.

He opens the passenger door to my car and waits for me to sit down. I buckle up as he comes around the back to the driver's side. "We have two more stops tonight. You up for it?"

I'm actually exhausted, but I'm not telling him. I want retracing my steps to be over and done with. "Sure."

He starts the car and takes off out of the parking lot. I squeeze my eyes and try to remember, but nothing shows up. It baffles me how my mind refuses to grant me access to parts of my brain.

I'm glad I have Mace to help me, but I'm not sure what to make of him. He's both charming and frustrating. On one hand, he seems to care about me and wants to protect me. On the other, he's a wild card that could turn on me at any moment. For now, I'm stuck on this ride with him, and I need to make the most of it while I can.

Chapter 5 The Bluffs

Mace

Lola's Maserati Gran Tourismo handles like a cheetah on the prowl. A slight tap on the gas and it explodes like a rocket, smooth like glass and faster than any other car on the road. Sexy red leather seats and the sleek console beg me to push her limits. Lola doesn't want to get pulled over by the cops, and she clenched up at seventy, so I keep it under eighty on the highway. First chance we get, we're taking this baby to the desert to break a hundred. This car can probably reach one-twenty in eight seconds. It's bored with twenty-five mile per hour speed limits. This car wants to soar like it was designed to do.

Kinda like Lola.

Her inner lioness is dying to come out. She has the shoes, the car, and the attitude. The way she let loose and danced with me was such a turn on. That's the kind of girl I could spend hours with, teasing her, making her laugh, making her crazy, watching her recover, and doing it all over again.

In the midst of my thoughts, I went the wrong way and missed the turn for the Golden Gate. Luckily there's a junction I can take that will swing us around the other way.

"Where're we going?"

Of course Lola noticed my change in direction. That's something she probably never does. She probably has her route all mapped out. Never misses an exit or uses a junction to reverse course. Well, I'm driving tonight, babe, and I take the long route.

She forgets her question as we ascend into the fog surrounding the bridge.

"Whoa." Her face lights up, and she looks stunning with her ultra sexy hair and makeup.

"Didn't you grow up here?"

"It's always pretty, but this is incredible. The fog is so thick. Like we're floating."

"Yeah. Cool." It's a beautiful sight. The jet black vehicle, the aged metal of the iconic red structure, and a ghostly blanket of fog so thick we can't see the cars in front of us or behind us.

I probably wouldn't have thought about it twice if she hadn't brought it up, but now that she has, I see it from her perspective.

As we exit the other side of the bridge, we're greeted with the winding streets of downtown San Francisco. I take her to an upscale Italian restaurant off Lombard Street on Telegraph Hill. "I love this restaurant."

"I know. After you went to the nightclub, you stopped here for dinner. Alone."

"I did?"

"Shall we go in and see if it triggers any memories?"

She looks down. "I can't go in there dressed like this."

"You did. Wearing exactly that. You sat at a table all by yourself and confidently ordered a meal."

Her gaze focuses on the entrance to the restaurant. Does she have the same courage tonight, or has she lost her mojo with her title as a cop?

"Fine. Let's go."

Good girl. "You can wear my jacket."

She doesn't answer, but I drop it over her shoulders as we enter. The hostess gives us a table and asks for our drink orders.

She looks at Lola first. "Iced tea."

"Whiskey neat."

Lola raises her hand and leans forward. "You know what? I'll have a whiskey sour."

That a girl. Ordered herself a mixed drink. Looked cute as hell doing it. Proud to be here to see it.

"So what is it you like here that's so good you'd come by yourself?" I ask her.

"Probably the chicken cannoli. Although the white lasagne calls my name quite often too."

"Mmm. And why didn't you bring a friend here? A girlfriend or a date?"

"Obviously I've lost my memory so I don't know why, but it's not something unusual for me. If I want the food, I go for it. I don't need to call someone and ask them to go with me. I just drive up and sit by myself. I'm pretty good company." She shrugs and smiles.

"You are. I'm just thinking there's a lot of men who would love to have dinner with you like this."

"Maybe." She looks out the window to avoid my scrutiny. I'm on to something here, so I'm not giving up.

"Even Griffin seems like he wants to be on your dance card. What's the story with that guy?"

Her gaze slides back to mine, and she's changed to a more relaxed and open version of Lola. "Griffin was the son of my dad's business partner. My dad ran the seminars. Griffin's dad sold them vitamins. We grew up together. Two children of celebrities on the road. We didn't have much else in common and when my dad died, we had nothing in common. Except his dad wanted to continue to profit off my dad's name, which didn't work at all. I stayed with him for too long because I thought my dad would want it. I planned on marrying him. It was on my life board."

The waitress returns with our drinks. Lola orders the white lasagne and smiles when I order the chicken cannoli.

"What's a life board?" I ask her after the waitress leaves.

"It was my dad's claim to fame. He held huge seminars where people created life boards. Images of their goals. Visualizing your future."

After I'm done laughing and she's done scowling at me, I say, "Life boards suck."

"True. If I'd followed mine, I'd be married to Griffin by now."

"Why'd you break up?"

"He was doing drugs. Caught him with cocaine and paraphernalia in his car. I'm a cop. I couldn't be associated with someone like that. So I broke up with him. He didn't take it well as you can see. He still checks on me. Says we're best friends."

"And yet you didn't call him to come get you from the hospital?"

"No."

"Hmm."

Our food arrives, and we eat in easy silence for a bit. She shares a few stories about her job and the restaurant. The food is really good, and I understand why she loves this place.

"Enough about me. So how do you like being part of a big family? How many kids have your parents adopted now?"

My family is a sore spot between us, so I'm glad she's willing to talk about it. It's a start to healing the divide. "There's ten kids now. Eight adopted, two biological."

"That's amazing. I shouldn't ask this, and it's probably a horrible question, but do you sometimes wonder if they love the biological kids more than you? I mean, I'm sure they love you all the same, but as an adopted child, do you wonder?"

"That's actually a natural question, and all of us have contemplated it at various times in our lives. My parents insist they love us all equally. Period. And their actions back that up, but sometimes it's the kids who have trouble believing it. A lot of us were rejected by our bio parents or foster parents, so when Mila and Foster opened their arms to us, we were skeptical. There's a lot of rebelling and testing them." I lean forward and make eye contact with her. She takes in a deep breath and looks at me with anticipation like she's hanging on every word. "I can tell you one thing I know for sure. Mila and Foster always come through for us, and they refuse to give us any legit reason to doubt their love. After a while, you begin to accept it." I shrug and take another mouthful of food.

"Wow. That's the most I've ever heard you talk about emotions and relationships."

"I can do it. It's not easy for me, but we have check-ins. We communicate a lot. Sometimes it's too much, and I have to get away, but I always come back." Once again I realize how lucky I am to have them in my life. "You don't have any family at all?"

"No. My mom died, and I never met her family. My dad was an only child. Griffin and his dad were the closest I had to family. Oh, and I have three half-siblings."

She stops talking and focuses on her food. We've wandered into dangerous territory because those three kids are part of the reason her father went to jail. He abandoned them and never paid child support.

We avoid that topic and a few others as we finish eating. She's smiling when the waitress takes our plates away and asks if we want dessert.

"Oh no. I'm stuffed. It was delicious. Thank you."

This is her happy place, and I'm glad I brought her here. She's even more entrancing when she's light-hearted and happy.

When the bill arrives, I glance at it but don't pick it up right away. There's something going on here, and I don't feel the urge to bolt from the table like I usually do anytime I'm forced to sit in one place for too long. I could enjoy the view with Lola for another hour or two.

Actually, Lola is working her way under my skin, and that means we have to go right this second.

I pick up the check and put my card in the fold, holding it up to urge the waitress to come quickly. I can't get comfortable around Lola. I'm helping her remember her shit, and then I'm clearing out. I have bad guys to catch, towns to roll through, hearts to break.

Lola's eyes widen when I stand quickly and walk toward the hostess with the bill in my hand. I hear her mutter, "Okay" behind me, but I'm not taking the time to explain this to her. Not sure I can explain it to myself.

***

After dinner, I drive her up to the bluffs above the Bay Bridge and park at the end of a cul-de-sac. This bridge is far less sexy than the Golden Gate, but it still gives off cool light patterns that reflect on the water. The wind bites my cheeks as I get out and start walking. I motion for her to come with me, but she waves me off and stays in the car.

We aren't here so I can stand on this cliff. She needs to come out here to trigger her memories. The fact she doesn't want to do it is a clue it could be crucial to what happened.

I march over and open the passenger door. "Why aren't you getting out?"

"It's cold." She shakes her head and purses her lips.

"You can wear my jacket."

"No. I don't want anything of yours, and I don't want to be here with you. Let's go." She tries to pull the door shut, but I force it open.

"Are you drunk?" Her sudden mood swing has me guessing.

"I'm not drunk. Leave me alone, Mace. This is way over the line." Her voice is a little slurred, but I believe her when she says she's not drunk. She only drank half of her drink. The most she feels is a little buzz.

"I'm not doing anything except asking you to do what you did before all by yourself. Why can't you do it if I'm here?"

She glares up at me. "This is where I come to talk to my dad."

Oh shit. Her dad. Sensitive topic. "And you think I'm responsible for his death, so you don't want me here?"

"I don't think it. I know it."

She's still holding onto that bullshit? "You're wrong." I slam the door shut and turn away from her. I don't need to defend my actions. I did my job and brought the guy in. Her dad got himself killed. Not my fault.

I spin around and open the door again. "We are here to trigger your memories. This is the last place I followed you to. Now I'd like you to go out there and do whatever you did so you can fill the damn holes in your brain, and we can avoid visiting a drug lord named Diablo."

"We? You're going with me after Diablo?"

"You're not going in alone."

"Huh." She shakes her head and steps out of the car. I wrap my jacket around her shoulders, and her fingers reach up to pull the jacket closed as she walks away from me. I give her some space and lean against the car as she closes her eyes, tilts her head down, and her back heaves with her sigh.

I've never regretted bringing in a criminal. Now that she's a cop, she must understand that it's part of the job. Maybe not, but for the first time, she's making me think about the fallout. From her perspective, I took away the father she loved. From mine, he was a druggie loser who deserved justice.

Her feet and legs are bare, but she doesn't shiver in the chilly wind. She stands strong and lets it buffet her. It's been a long time, but we need to clear the air about her dad.

She turns and marches past me with her head down and arms crossed. I manage to grab hold of her hand, but she keeps walking until our arms are both stretched out and we are as far apart as we can be while still touching.

I pull her back and she resists. With a stronger tug, she stumbles backward until she's next to me. She tries to pull her hand away, but I move our locked palms behind her back and pull her up against me.

She gasps and looks up at me with shuttered eyes.

"I'm sorry he died."

She flinches back and looks away.

"I didn't know about your dad's drug connections."

Her head snaps back and she stares into my eyes. "What connections?"

"You don't know?"

"No. Tell me."

"The rumor was your dad was going to snitch on some influential people, so he got killed."

"I've never heard this before."

"Really? I thought it was common knowledge."

"No. Nobody told me. His death was a hit job?"

"That's the way I understood it."

Her face freezes then her forehead falls onto my shoulder. "No."

I don't say anything as she starts to cry, but I put another hand on her back and pull her closer. "I'm sorry."

"He wasn't a bad person."

"People are complicated. We're not all good or all bad. We just make dumb choices sometimes."

She nods and wipes her eyes. "Let's go back."

"One more minute." I like her pressed up close to me like this. She's vulnerable and soft. She looks hot in that dress, and I want to keep her in it a little longer before she turns back into blue-striped anchor girl with her tight headbands and organized life.

My hands force her closer without any conscious effort from myself. I'm responding to something beyond my control when my lips brush hers.

She stiffens and sucks in a long slow breath. Her body goes rigid in my arms, and she weakly tries to pull away. That only makes me want to draw her closer and seal the kiss.

The plush pillow of her lips smashes softly as I kiss her fully. She's still tentative, but my body is committed to it. I lick her lips to get her to open for me, but she growls. I flick my tongue over her lips again and run my hand up her back, pressing her tits to my chest. "C'mon, babe. Let go for a second. I got you."

The fight in her eyes leaves her, and she melts with a sigh, giving me her weight and forcing me to hold her up. Our tongues battle, and we kiss like long-lost lovers. She groans into my mouth, and my already hard dick twitches toward her core. This is why I never forgot her. This is also what terrified me at age twenty and still freaks me out now. She flips from proper and fighting it one second to lighting up like she did when she was an eighteen-year-old virgin. It still turns me on like a drug. It's this secret part of her she keeps shrouded, and I'm the only one who can bring it out. I can't imagine Griffin ever kissed her this way.

With no warning she stiffens and pulls away. As abruptly as the switch flipped on, it's out like a light.

"Um..." She wipes her lips with the back of her hand. "Not part of the recreation, I take it."

"No. Last time I didn't get close to you. I watched from my truck."

"Then we should stop. This can't help."

"I'm not trying to refresh your memories. I'm trying to create new ones."

She shakes her head. "No. Mace. I'm not falling for that again. For all I know you made this whole thing up, and you're trying to get in on my case."

She seriously thinks I'd fake this entire thing? "I don't need to be in on your action. I take better paying gigs than a cop." Pfft. Cops make one tenth what the average bounty hunter makes, and I'm way above average.

She breaks out of my arms and scowls at me. "Are we done?"

"For tonight we are. Yeah."

"No. I mean are we done retracing my steps? Because it didn't trigger my memory, and if you don't have anywhere else to take me then we're done." She steps back toward the car slowly. "So, goodbye, Mace. Thank you for this. It helped, but I'll take it from here."

"That kiss must've really touched a nerve if you're running away from it like this."

"No. It wasn't the kiss. I'm unphased by that."

She's lying. It bothered her. She hates it that she wants and needs me so badly. "You need help figuring out who put an explosive on your garage door."

"I'll do that on my own." Now she's being obstinate, saying no to me to prove her point. I get it, but it's reckless and self-destructive.

"You gonna go after Diablo alone?" Not practical at all. She's already admitted she has no one to help her.

"None of your business." She stomps back to the car and folds into the passenger seat.

I get in and keep quiet as she huffs and stares out her window. If she doesn't want me around, fine. I'm back on the trail I was on. I didn't lose too much time, and I don't need to take on Loralei's headaches.

I start the car and skid out on the bluffs as we take off down the hill.

***

As we enter her neighborhood in Sausalito, I notice a car that pulled out from the side of the road when we drove by.

He gets right up on my bumper and blasts his high beams.

This car rides low, and the lights land right in my eyes, blocking my vision.

I veer left, he follows. I veer right, same thing. "We got a tail."

Loralei looks out the back window. "He probably wants to race. Happens all the time with this car."

The tail behind us accelerates and hits our bumper, causing Loralei's head to jerk.

"Happens all the time, huh? Hold on."

I floor it, and the Maserati responds like supercharged lighting. The tail speeds up too, but there's no way to catch us. I pull off some extra turns, the wheels skidding out behind me. The other car follows but further back now.

We make a right onto a dark road. I pull over and kill all the lights.

Loralei is breathing heavy as the other car races past us. I turn the Maserati around with the lights off and head back to her house. "Get some stuff. You're coming with me."

She laughs. "No."

"You're not safe there. An explosion and getting run off the road in the same day? You're a target."

"That was just kids lighting fireworks and some jerk who wanted to race. Nothing more. I really didn't peg you as the paranoid type."

I open her garage from the bottom of the hill. No explosion. I pull inside and close the door. "Go pack some shit. Bring any weapons and gear you'll need. I'll take you up to Twist Cabins to keep you safe."

"I'm not going anywhere with you, and I'm definitely never going back to Twist Cabins." She shakes her head and rolls her eyes.

"You need a safe house. Go get your stuff or we're leaving now." I start the engine again and put the car in reverse. "You sure you want that nightie to be all you'll have to wear? Won't bother me one bit, but my brothers will get an eyeful of you."

She growls and pushes her door open. "Fine." She thrusts her long legs out and down. She stops and points back at me. "You can leave now." Her voice is muffled through the glass, but I can read her lips.

I turn off the car and stick my head out my side. "Get in the car. We're leaving."

"I'm not going to Twist Cabins. I'm not a target, and you are not my supervisor. Goodbye." She waves over her shoulder and inserts her house key into the inner garage door.

As I watch her long-ass legs move, I have a choice to make again. Walk away and let her handle this on her own or keep getting tangled deeper with Loralei. She's bad news. She hates me, and I can't trust her.

I'm done recreating her memories. I'm free to leave. Got a job to get back to that pays really well.

I tap the dash of the car a few times. Last time I left her she got kidnapped. This time I know the danger.

I'm staying.

Chapter 6 Wicked

I walk in on her holding one heel in her hand while she's bending and frowning as she pulls off the other shoe. "Are you still here?"

"Unfortunately."

She places her shoes neatly on a rack by the door and walks into her bedroom. "Your time, your dime."

She leaves me standing in her living room. When I hear the shower run, it's my chance to take a look around. The place is immaculate like a model home. Nothing but navy blue, white, and gold nautical decor, obnoxiously healthy houseplants, one lonely shiny laptop on her desk in the corner. Where's the mess? Where's the mail? I should whip through here like a tornado and move everything out of place just to piss her off, but I won't. She's having a rough time. I'm not going to add to it out of spite.

Pictures of her with her father adorn the walls of the hallway. One of her looking smart in a police uniform, but conspicuously alone after her father's death. I tap her bedroom door, and it slowly swings open. Whoa. Hello. Have I teleported to another house? No nautical stuff in here. The bed is covered in deep cranberry velvet with animal print black and brown silk sheets. Mirrors over the headboard and recessed lighting make it look like the set of a porn movie. Thick black and brown shag rugs cover deep walnut hardwood floors. No houseplants in here. Only two tall twisted iron lamps stand next to the bed.

Well, well, well. Officer Valentine has a secret wicked side. I knew it from the second I saw her leopard heels. She's a walking contradiction.

In her dresser, I find her gun case. The key is predictably taped to the bottom. I open it and take out a shiny new Glock with her initials engraved into the grip. Also not what I expected from my straight and narrow nemesis. She has ammo too, so I take the time to load it.

"Hold it right there. Hands up." She's aiming a gun at me, her legs spread wide, arms forward, while wearing a towel and nothing else. Steam from the shower dissipates over the second towel that's twisted up on her head. "Put the gun down."

"Relax. I'm prepping it in case whoever tried to kill you tonight comes back." My gaze scans her towel, which is bursting at the edges, trying to stay gripped to her curves, but I can tell it really wants to fall to the floor.

She frowns and looks down at herself. A slight blush tinges her cheeks, but she shakes it off. "No one tried to kill me."

"Semantics." I shrug and take one last look at her spread thighs before I finally pull my eyes away to finish loading the cartridge.

"Put the weapon on the bed."

I chuckle at the hard edge in her voice. She's wary of me but not the people who might be out to get her? "I like your bad cop in a towel routine. It's sexy."

"It's not a routine. I am a bad cop, and you don't want to see what I do to perps who don't cooperate so put the gun down."

The gun sinks into the plush fabric of her bedspread as I turn to face her with my hands up. "Are you gonna arrest me,

MEMORIZING MACE

officer?" I swipe my tongue over my lower lip and her eyes trace it.

Her hands shake as she lowers the gun. "No."

"Aww, c'mon. This was getting fun."

She sets her gun down and stares at me with her mouth open. She grips her towel and looks around for something to wear. She hastily throws on a white silk robe and works the towel out from underneath without giving me a peek at any skin. "Get out, Mace."

Uh, no. Not leaving. "We'll take shifts guarding the front door."

"Really not necessary."

"Abundance of caution."

"I—" A knock at the door cuts her off, and she tilts her head toward the sound.

We both grab our guns and pace to the front of the house. She checks the peephole and relaxes her shoulders. "It's Griffin."

"So?" I keep my gun pointed at the door.

"He's harmless. Really."

"Fine." As I'm lowering my gun, she hands me hers before unlocking the door.

"You seriously have a peephole? Who does that anymore?"

"I do."

"It's old fashioned and useless. Get a camera."

She growls and points down the hall. "Go put the guns away, and I'll get rid of him." She bends over to release her hair from the towel and tightens up her robe.

I back up and perch behind the door. No matter what she says, I'm not leaving her alone with him.

"Griffin." She fakes a smile. "What're you doing here?"

"Who's that guy you were with?"

All my muscles tighten as the douchebag brings me up right away.

"That's really none—"

"Is he your bodyguard?" His voice is high-pitched and amped up like he's high.

"What? No."

"Are you dating him? Because really, Loralei, not at all your type."

"I'm not dating him." She grits her teeth and glances at me. I'm too busy holding back my impulse to pulverize him, so I can't tell her anything with my eyes. But she sees something in mine, and her brows draw together.

"What the hell is going on with you? You disappear for weeks and come back with that guy? He looks like one of the guys you lock up, not someone you hang out with."

"Hey!" Her head snaps back to him and her spine stiffens.

"Greasy long hair. Probably a druggie. That guy'll give you an STD. Let me in."

I take a step forward, but Loralei stops me with her palm flat. She forces Griffin deeper out on the porch. "No. Let me tell you something. That *guy* has more empathy and compassion in his pinky finger than you'll ever dream of having. That *guy* buries you when it comes to being faithful to his family out of love and honor, not money or fame." She's spitting the words out now, her voice scratching. "And that *guy* could school you on female anatomy and how to rock my world in bed to the point I'm screaming his name. So get gone and don't come around here anymore talking your crap you know nothing about, or I'll have him show you exactly what he can do."

Her words stun me. I had no idea she saw me that way. I knew we had amazing sex once a long time ago, but I didn't realize she thinks I'm compassionate or faithful. Once again, Loralei has blown my mind.

"Jeez, Loralei. Relax. He's just some loser you're boning. Another one will be along soon."

That's it. Time for me to face this bozo and send him packing. With the two guns in my waistband fully visible, I step out next to Loralei and stare Griffin-the-douchebag down.

I wrap an arm around her and pull her close till my lips hit her temple. Griffin looks on like he's just seen Bigfoot kiss his ex-girlfriend. "Problem, babe?"

"Nope. Bye, Griffin." She wiggles her fingers at him.

Griffin looks me up and down, and I can almost see his dick shrivel up as he steps back. "Uh, yeah. Bye."

We watch him walk to his car before I pull her in the door and close and lock it behind us. I keep my arm around her neck and smile.

"Wow. That was..."

I interrupt her with a spontaneous kiss. She stiffens, but her lips are soft and warm from her shower. She smells like flowers. My tongue swipes her lower lip. This knocks her out of her daze, and she opens for me. Her hands come up and squeeze my shoulders.

She grunts as I push her back up against the door and press my hard dick into the soft fabric of her robe.

I'm expecting her to stop me, but she doesn't. Her hands run down my back and land on my ass, shoving my hips deeper into her.

I growl and dive into the kiss, grinding into her and smashing her harder against the door. I grab one luscious tit and squeeze it in my palm. It's heavy and round and feels incredible. "You're fascinating, you know? Quite the contradiction. Tame to wild. Innocent to wicked."

She moans then stiffens and slowly pushes me off. "I, uh, lost control there. I'm not wicked. I'm really not. We should uh..." She's breathing heavy and her eyes have darkened. "Stop."

"All right. Up to you." I back away with my hands up. Her gaze travels to my pants where she can see the two guns and my hard dick. Yeah, that's what you're missing out on, Lola.

Pulling back nearly kills me, but I'm honoring her verbal request to stop. Her body clearly wants to keep going. I can see her hard nipples through her robe. "You can arrest me now, ya know, officer. If you want to."

She shakes her head and laughs. Her hand runs through her hair. "No. Not doing that. Goodnight, Mace."

She scrambles away to her wicked red bedroom.

I'm chuckling as I take a seat on the couch.

Yep, a walking contradiction, that girl. She makes my balls blue, and confuses the hell outta me. I kinda love it.

Chapter 7 Butt Dimples

Loralei

Mace is kissing me in the dark. It's the most rebellious thing I've ever done in my eighteen years on this planet. I'm Daddy's girl. I do what I'm told. I guess he never explicitly told me I couldn't sneak a boy into my room, but I'm sure it's implied in the rules.

But if my dad gets mad at me, it'll be worth whatever consequences I earn. Mace is gorgeous, he kisses like a movie star, and I want him to be my first. I'm leaving for college anyway. I'm going to be reckless for once in my life and take this chance.

"It's your turn, Lola."

God, his gravelly voice is so sexy, it vibrates in all my lady parts.

"Yes." I arch my back and tilt my head so his mouth can ravage my neck. I spread my legs and when his fingers dip under the waistband of my panties, I think I might explode.

"Mace." His name comes out in a scratchy growl. "Shh." I shush myself. "My dad will hear us."

"Your dad?" Mace's mouth pulls away slowly. I try to grab his neck and drag him back, but my fingers slip over his skin. "Are you awake?"

Oh shoot. That's not Mace's younger voice. It's his present day deep and raspy voice.

I open my eyes, and he's shirtless on top of me. His brows are drawn, and his mouth is turned down in a scowl. "I swear to God I thought you were awake."

"It looks like I wasn't." I shrug my shoulders. Oh man, this is bad.

"Shit. I'm sorry." He pulls his hand from inside my panties, which makes me sad because in my dream I loved it there. He rolls off me and lays on his side. He plants his elbow in the bed, his head resting on his palm. "Still wanna fuck?" A naughty grin turns up the side of his mouth.

"No. Is that what I said I wanted?"

"Yep. You begged me."

"Well, I didn't mean it."

"Sure."

I'm wet between my legs, and my heart is beating fast. If I were crazy like I used to be, I'd grab him and finish what we started. But that got me in a lot of trouble last time. I'm a responsible adult now. I've mastered self-control. I've also mastered self-stimulation to take the edge off, but Mace doesn't need to know about that.

"Mace. You took my virginity, got out of bed, and went and arrested my father before the sheets were cold. You think I'd ever repeat my mistake with you?"

"I won't arrest your father this time. Promise." He folds his hands together in prayer.

"No. Just no. Even if I'm begging you. No."

He flops down on his back, revealing a huge bulge in his boxer briefs that makes me gasp. "Your turn to watch the door." He rubs his eyes, and I can't help but stare at the taut skin that wraps around his bowling-ball like biceps.

I pull my gaze from his arms to check the clock. Four in the morning!

"Did anything happen?"

"No."

"Then I'm not getting out of bed."

"Fine." He rolls to his side next to me and pushes a wave of heat at me like I've just walked out of the air conditioning into the desert. Yet, it's humid too like he just took a shower. I catch a whiff of my own soap. Oh Lord. Mace was naked in my shower. How am I going to sleep next to him?

"Get out of my bed."

"Protecting you," he mumbles.

"Protect me from the couch."

But he's already asleep, and there's no way I can move him out without a gun, so I drop my head on my pillow and attempt to sleep with Mace Twist's massive body next to me in the bed.

***

In the morning, Mace is snoring on his back with his mouth slightly open, face relaxed. He didn't bother to climb under the sheets, so every inch of his toned, tan, and tattooed body is exposed for me to ogle. Coarse, dark hair covers his chest, arms, and legs along with a mess of tribal tattoos, waves, and Hawaiian flowers. The names of his family members are written in script all over his torso. A red Mom takes the spot over his heart. The others I need to get closer to examine.

Nothing on him is soft. He's like a giant superhero asleep next to me in my bed. I wish he wasn't such an asshole because sex with him would be phenomenal. My body still tingles from my half-dream half-reality makeout session I had last night where I was eighteen again and sneaking him into my room. I can't get over the idea that dream-man Mace was actually real-world Mace thinking he had permission to tuck his hand into my panties.

Kissing him as an adult is much more intense than I remember, and it was the experience of my lifetime up until yesterday. Now Mace is older, he's even more confident and skilled. I wonder what new tricks he's learned since we were together that one night. He has this magical way of making me act out desires I've buried deep inside. Unfortunately, nothing we've done has triggered my memory, and I haven't forgotten how he hurt me.

My phone pings on the dresser. It's a text from Helix saying I have a meeting with Diablo this afternoon. A tinge of anxiety runs through me, but I have to be brave. He could hold the answers to everything. Why was I on the island? Did Arthur kidnap me? Who forced me to take drugs? I know I'd never do it voluntarily.

I scramble out of bed and rush to my laptop, leaving Mace snoozing behind me. I only have a few hours to find out all I can about this Diablo person.

At two p.m., I'm researching an idea to hack into his phone when Mace finally emerges from my bedroom. He stands in the hallway, rubbing his face and scratching his balls. My eyes bug out seeing him standing in his briefs and nothing else. Having Mace walking around my house half-naked is messing with my focus.

Seeing him at the hospital shook me. His dancing at the club gave me tremors, but his gargantuan body kissing me in my bed exploded my world. I'm off my game. This isn't good.

I tear my eyes from his ripped abs and focus on my work.

"Got any booze?" His voice sounds like sandpaper.

MEMORIZING MACE 75

"No."

"Beer?"

"No. Coffee." I point to the kitchen.

He grunts and slides his feet on the floor as he walks in there. His briefs hang low on his hips showing off two massive dimples above the curves of his butt. I bite my lip and look away again. No. No, Loralei. No Mace. He's bad. Yes, his ass is a work of art created by God, but he's the bad guy.

Right? Gah!

Mace trods back in with a mug and plops down on my couch, throwing his feet up on the coffee table again like he did last night. The man has no manners. "Any word from Helix?" he asks me, finally tuning into the situation.

"Nothing you need to know." I dismiss him and keep my eyes on my work.

"Did you hear from him?" His voice perks up.

I reply with a resting bitch face to let him know I'm not answering him.

"What're you working on?"

When I don't respond, he looks at his own phone. "Three o'clock? It's two now. When were you gonna wake me up?" He must've received a message from Helix too.

"I wasn't. You're not invited. It's a meeting for me."

"Do you know who this guy is?"

"Spent the day researching it. Looks like he's very wealthy and runs a boxing gym. Probably as a front for his drug and money laundering op, but no one has nailed him for it yet."

"It's much more serious than that. I'm going with you." He stands and walks to the front door.

"Not necessary, Mace. Thank you. Really. I'm done with you. You didn't follow me to the meeting last time. You're not coming this time."

He doesn't listen and marches out the front door in his underwear and bare feet. A few minutes later, he returns with a bunch of clothes over his arm and starts dressing right in my living room. Watching him dress is almost as fun as watching him undress. His long limbs sliding into his pants and shirt. The masculine way he buttons his jeans. His beautiful hair swinging in his face and over his shoulder as he adjusts.

"You ready to meet with the Devil?"

I stand and prop my fingers on the desk. "I don't want you to come with me."

He stares at me with his jaw tight, hands on his hips, one knee cocked. "Okay. I'm gonna tell you what you need to hear. The dude is a heavy player in a Venezuelan cartel. He's a mobster. He has connections everywhere, and there's a long list of hit men waiting in line to make him happy. If that involves taking you out, he could have it done with a wink in your direction."

"I know this. You mentioned it, and I've been researching him. I have a plan. If I can get access to his phone..."

"No. Your plan is bringing me with you. You know why? Because he knows who I am. He may be El Diablo but I'm the Volcano. Not a hit man, but a bounty hunter you don't want to see coming after you. The Volcano catches you, throws you in the lava, and tortures you all the way to the police station. He will not mess with me. Not if he wants to live."

There's a lot of information to unpack there. Mace is known for torturing his skips, and the head of a drug cartel knows who he is. He's the Volcano, which seems fitting as he's Hawaiian, tall and dark, and looks like he could blow without warning. I've underestimated Mace all these years. I should've known he'd be larger than life in his career too. I have to admit, it's sexy. Totally illegal, but definitely changes the way I see him. It would also be unwise of me to go see Diablo without the Volcano at my back.

"All right. You can come with me."

He throws his hands up. "Hallelujah. She sees the light."

"Let me get ready, and I'll tell you my plan in the car." I close my laptop and head to my room to dress. I know exactly what I'm going to wear. A tailored suit with an inner pocket to disguise my gun.

"No plans," he calls out behind me. "Plans always get fucked."

Chapter 8 One-Way Street

"You sure you don't want to hear my plan?" Mace and I are parked in the alley behind Rios Fitness and Boxing center in Oakland.

Mace has his eyes on the entrance. "No. Wing it. Always."

"Just let me lead. All right?" I let him drive my Maserati again, but now that we're here, I need to be in charge.

His gaze slices to mine. "Sure."

Mace doesn't seem like the type to let anyone else lead, so I take his promise with a grain of salt. My skin itches, and my heart's pumping pure adrenaline. Maybe he's right. We should wing it. We don't know what's going to happen and having a plan doesn't guarantee anything, just makes your expectations too high.

"Let's do this."

We enter through the back door and catch the attention of some guys working out with weights. "You lost?"

I'm about to answer when Mace starts talking. "Where's Diablo?"

The guys chuckle and point down a hallway to our left. They are pretty brave to laugh at nearly seven-foot-tall Mace. I walk in front of Mace to an office at the end of the long hallway. Mace peeks into a room with the door half open. A fan runs in the corner, and there's another door out the back that I'd guess leads to the alley. We've walked around in a big U from our car.

I didn't see him at first, but a tall man with salt and pepper hair steps into my field of vision. He's wearing a white suit with a black shirt and a nice watch. He checks out Mace and I for a long moment before offering us seats. "Loralei, you brought a friend?"

"Volcano," Mace answers curtly. "Nice to meet ya."

Diablo's neck stiffens, and he slows his movements as he sits down, his eyes glued to Mace. "*The* Volcano?"

"That's me."

"Ahh. I haven't had the pleasure of working with you, but I hear you're the best."

Mace nods, and Diablo slowly turns his attention to me. His face is appropriately pale for someone who has just encountered the legendary Volcano.

"What can I do for you?" he asks me.

"I was hoping that, ya know, the issue we discussed last time, we could talk about it again." Of course I have no idea what I asked him last time, so I don't want to be too specific.

He scuffs awkwardly. "You'd like to talk about Arthur Morganna?"

Shoot. I should've figured that based on what Helix told me. Now I've gone and asked him about a man who died since the last time I saw him.

I'm stumbling through trying to say something to salvage the conversation, but Mace butts in. "No. Actually, I wanted to ask you about Giselle. You seen her?"

"Giselle?"

What the heck? Mace just threw a curveball at both of us. Why didn't he tell me he was going to ask about Giselle?

"I heard she's out of the country. Mourning for Arthur." Diablo's voice shakes, and his hand reaches into his jacket pocket. I tense, preparing for him to draw a gun, but Mace stays calm.

He leans in and puts his forearm on Diablo's desk. "Well you'll be sure to tell her Volcano's looking for her. All right?"

Oh shoot. That's clearly a threat. I was hoping to keep this friendly with Diablo and get on his good side, not goad him into a fight.

Diablo partially stands and his eyes jitter. Mace spooked him. "I might have her number. Let me go look in my car." He straightens and reaches for the back door.

Mace stands too. "Where you going, Diablo? You're not skipping out on us. Are you?" He steps around the desk and his hands come out like he's about to swipe at Diablo.

Diablo races out the back door, and Mace juts out after him. I'm following behind when I see a puff of white smoke hit Mace's face. He doubles over with his eyes closed tight. "Ah, shit."

"What is that?"

"It burns like hell. Let's chase him."

"What? But your eyes."

"I'll be okay." He swipes at his eyes with his sleeve. "You drive." He throws me the keys. "Follow him or we'll never see him again."

"All right. Get in."

Mace walks with hunched shoulders to the passenger seat. "Goddamn mutherfucker."

"We should take care of you first."

"Follow him!"

A black Mercedes tears out of the alley, and I'm sure that's him. My Maserati can catch up to him, no problem. "Here." I throw a water bottle at Mace and ram the car into gear. The wheels squeal, the exhaust roars, and we're at sixty miles per hour in less than three seconds.

I catch up to the Mercedes two blocks down the street. Mace is splashing the water on his face and squinting through the windshield to try to see what's happening.

The Mercedes turns right going the wrong way down a one-way street. I slam on the breaks.

"Why'd you stop?"

"It's a one-way street."

"So? Go!"

"I can't go the wrong way down a one-way street!"

"Yes you fucking can. Follow him."

As much as I want to, I can't. My feet and hands will not let me drive this car the wrong way down a one-way street. We peel out and blaze down to the next block. "We'll get him down here."

"No you won't. He's long gone."

Mace is right. There's no sign of Diablo's Mercedes. We lost him. I pull over into the bike lane and park the car. The adrenaline that was coursing through me suddenly starts boiling. I am literally on fire like Diablo threw cocaine at me instead of Mace. My fingernails dig into the leather of the steering wheel. I check the car again to make sure I'm in park on the side of the road and then close my eyes.

Like someone smacked me with a club, my memories come flooding back. The one-way street sign. I've seen it before. I've gone the wrong way down that street before, but I wasn't driving. Diablo was.

"Oh my God."

"What?" Mace rips his shirt off and wipes his face with a clean part of it.

I want to help him, but my mind is in freefall.

Images on a white screen flash through my head so fast, I only catch parts of scenes. But I know in my heart it was real. I can feel everything that happened before and after even if I can't see it.

Diablo kidnapped me. We drove the wrong way down that same street. Fast. I was terrified. He told me everything as I sat in the backseat of the same Mercedes we were just following. My hands were bound. He knew my dad. I was asking too many questions. Arthur Morganna had a job for me. He said I was lucky to get to work for Morganna instead of getting killed.

"Lola, tell me what's going on."

I hide my face in my hands, but it won't stop the deluge. I can't talk. The fear is paralyzing me. I'm feeling it all again like it's happening now. He grabbed me from behind. I fought. He punched me and subdued my hands and legs. He threatened to kill me as he threw me in the car. He drove us to the harbor. He said he was sorry for what happened to my dad. He said I'd like it at Morganna's island.

"A boat." I manage to mumble out the two words.

"What boat?"

"He kidnapped me. Took me to his boat. We sailed to Morganna's island and oh my God. No!"

"You're remembering?"

"It's playing like a movie on a white screen. I can see it. I can feel it all again. I was terrified. Diablo was fronting as friendly, but his words were deadly."

"You remember the island?" Mace's voice is high and fast too. We're both excited and running on pure adrenaline.

"Yes! I remember Giselle. She was there. She welcomed me. Introduced me to Arthur with a smile. Said they were happy to see me. Acted like it was normal. God. I was so confused and scared."

"Did he hurt you?" he asks, deep and serious.

I shake my head. "Giselle shot a needle in my arm. I was euphoric. It felt so good. Oh my God. I did drugs and I liked it. But then it all got dark. I was in a room. They were gone. I felt like death. Giselle offered me more. I tried to say no, but she said it would make me feel better. They forced me to take the drugs. Then I woke up in the hospital."

When I look up, he's squinting at me, and his face is burning red like he's on fire. I need to get it together for him. My hands are shaking, but he needs me right now.

"I'm so sorry. Hold on. I'll take you somewhere to rinse that stuff off your face." I slam the car into gear and race through the streets to the first gas station I can find. I pull up to the air and water pumps and run around to Mace's side. Without thinking, I drop a quarter in the machine and open his door.

"Stop!" He holds his hands out, but it's too late. I already have the water hose in my hand.

I squeeze the water into his face and it dribbles down his chest. He shakes his head and closes his eyes. "Stop!" He swipes a long arm out and knocks the water hose out of my hand.

"I'm so sorry. I'm freaking out. Are you okay? I can't think straight. You need water on it."

"No more water."

"It's bleeding!" Red blotches fill the whites of his eyes like he's a demon possessed. I'm breathing so fast I think my heart is going to burst out of my chest. "We need to get you to a hospital."

"No. Just take me home. It's not bleeding."

Home. Mace's home. Twist Cabins. They hate me. "I can't do that."

"I'm fine. Get back in the car and take me up to Boulder Creek."

The last place in the world I want to go is Twist Cabins, but Mace helped me when I needed it, and it would be horrible of me to abandon him now. Maybe I could drop him off without being seen, but I really don't want to leave him like this. I don't know. My mind is racing.

He slumps in the passenger seat as I start the car again. He leans his chair back and covers his eyes with his forearm. "Mutherfucker threw cocaine in my face. Coward."

"I'm so sorry. I didn't want you to get hurt."

"Not your fault."

We sit in silent shock as I drive us to the highway as fast as I can without getting arrested.

Once we're headed south, he says, "You remember?"

I do and it's monumental, but I'm more worried about him. "How are your eyes?"

"The burning stopped. It's numb now. Tell me what you remember."

"I remember meeting with Helix about the missing girl. Her name is Hannah Clark. I wanted to talk with Morganna, but Helix said no. He said I could meet with Diablo instead and set it up. He kidnapped me. Was Helix in on it?"

"If he was, he's going to have an unpleasant run in with Volcano. Helix has been a friend of mine for a long time, but there's no trust amongst thieves. If he did this to you, I'll kill him."

"I don't know. I didn't get the sense he was in on it."

I'm trying to remember details from that night. Mace doing a striptease is not in my memory movie. "You didn't dance with me at Dragon Lounge the first time, did you?"

"Nope. Spur of the moment thing. I went off script. It happens."

That makes me chuckle. It happens to him, but not to me. "I remember sitting at the restaurant alone and feeling awkward in the dress, but talked myself out of caring what other people think."

"Good."

I'm having trouble keeping my eyes on the road and focusing on the new images too. "I went to the bluffs and the cold wind hit my face as I cried to my dad. I had no clue you were following me."

He nods. "I stayed back. Watched from a distance. You didn't seem like you were up to any trouble, so I left you there. Big mistake."

"I met with Diablo and he kidnapped me. Jeez. How could I forget that?" I smash my palm into my forehead.

"Your brain blocked it. Trauma."

"I guess so. God, the drugs were the worst. I felt like I was crawling out of my skin."

He rubs his eyes.

"Do you feel high from the cocaine in your eye?"

"No." He chuckles.

We're quiet for a while, and I turn the radio on. He reaches out and starts messing with the buttons, not settling on any one song.

"When we get home, you'll stay for your safety. Diablo will be after you."

His announcement drops like a boulder in my gut. "I can't stay at Twist Cabins. I'll find someplace else."

"You will stay with me in my cabin. You're not going anywhere alone. Not anymore."

It's nice of him to act like he cares about me, but we both know the truth. I'm not welcome at his family's refuge in the mountains. It's a deeply personal place for them, and they guard it carefully. Mace knows this deep down, and he may have temporarily forgotten, but he hates me for what I did to them. He doesn't even know the worst of it yet. If he finds out, he'll never talk to me again.

Chapter 9 Remy

Mace

The higher we climb in elevation the more confident I feel about my decision to bring her here. She'll be safe, and I'll have time to recover before I go after Diablo.

Lola, however, is white knuckling the steering wheel the closer we get to Twist Cabins. She pulls into the gravel parking lot and sighs. "We're here."

I reach for the door handle, but she doesn't move.

"I'll just stay here in the car."

"No you won't." My vision is still blurry, but I can see her face crumble when she looks at my eyes.

"Is it that bad?" I ask her.

"It's really red. I'm so torn. I want to help you with your eyes, but I can't face them. I just can't."

Looking up the hill, I don't see anyone outside, but my vision is compromised. "We go straight to my cabin. No one sees you, and they won't even know you're here."

She shakes her head, and her hands fall from the wheel. "I don't belong here."

"Listen." I lean over the console and bring a hand up to her cheek. "I want you to be with me right now. I need to recover, and I want you there. We'll deal with anything else later."

She blushes and looks down. Is it so hard for her to believe I want her around after all we've been through? "Okay."

I grin and we get out of the car. Luckily, we make it to my cabin unseen. My bed never looked so inviting before, and I plop down on my back.

"Can I get you some ice? A compress?" She stands next to the bed with a worried look on her face.

"Nah. It just needs time."

"I think we should rinse it out again so it doesn't get infected."

She's right. Good idea. I get up and run my eyes under the sink. The numbness is wearing off, and blood covers most of the white part of my right eye. My left eye was barely hurt. "It looks worse than it feels."

She stands behind me looking at my eyes in the mirror. "It looks like crap. Do you have any eye drops?"

"No. Nothing. My mom might have something."

She stiffens and backs up. "I can go hide if you want your mom to come look at it."

"You don't need to hide. Especially from my mom. She's the kindest soul you've ever met. She was offering to drive up and take care of you when you were in the hospital."

"Oh. Wow. That's nice of her."

"I can't promise my brothers will be so forgiving, but my mom? No worries." I plop down on the bed again, and she sits next to me.

I take her hand in mine. "I'm glad you got your memory back."

She looks down and nods. "Not sure it helps the mess I've created."

"We don't know yet how it helps, but at least we know your brain isn't permanently broken. That has to feel good."

She leans over me with one arm propped to my side. "Thank you for helping me get my memory back. You didn't have to."

I lift her chin with my hand. "I wanted to do it. I wanted to help you regain your memory and not just because I felt sorry for you. I wanted you to feel like yourself again, so I can spend some time with you. I like it when you smile."

"Oh."

"Come lie down with me." She stares at my hand patting the bed like I've offered her poison. "You've been through a lot today."

Her brows twist, and her lips mash together like she's pondering the great paradox. On the one hand, she has this big strong warm body to cuddle up to, and she knows she needs it after today. On the other hand, she's still claiming to hate me. "I shouldn't."

"You're as worn out as me. It's just a nap. Nothing more. Don't overthink it."

"You and I are not friends. We can't lie in a bed together."

I have a solution for that. "Remember our deal? I help you get your memory back, you forgive me. Therefore, we are no longer enemies, and you can lay down in my bed with me without guilt."

She exhales and smiles like I've given her permission she needed but couldn't give herself. She climbs in next to me, keeping a modest distance, but I still have her hand and pull her up onto my chest. She tenses but doesn't stop me. "So. Your brain downloaded some brutal stuff on you today."

"Yeah." She settles her head on my pec, and her hand lays flat on my abs. Holding her like this feels nice.

"If you need to talk, I have time." Talking isn't usually my thing, but I like hearing what Loralei has to say.

She relaxes and snuggles closer. "I'm still grappling with it. I'm so worried about your eye."

"I'm gonna be okay. You remembered you were kidnapped and drugged. It's gotta be messing with you."

She nods. "I hate that I fell for it. I should've known better with Diablo. Why didn't I fight harder when Giselle tried to drug me?" Her voice is tight with her frustration.

"Don't blame yourself. Nothing you could've done." I rub her back to offer some support.

"I walked right into it. I should've planned it better. Have someone back me up. I was being overconfident, trying to prove myself."

"Been there. Done that." My hand comes up to caress her hair. It's silky and thick and smells like chocolate.

"I was terrified on the boat to the island. He talked to me in this soothing tone, but the stuff he said was diabolical."

"Like what?"

She props her chin on her hand so she can look up at me. "He said it was a shame what happened to my father. I was shocked he brought it up. What's his connection to my dad? I'll have to research it."

"We can ask Helix, but probably drugs."

"Yeah. In my mind, I keep seeing Diablo smiling and saying I'd love working with Arthur Morganna. No sarcasm either. He truly believed I'd love it. He didn't once consider my choice or decision in the matter. I should've knocked him out, but I didn't make a move. I was in shock, and his cordiality threw me."

"That's okay. He's a master manipulator. Don't feel bad for falling for it."

"We got there, and it was so weird. Like this tropical island in the middle of nowhere. I met Giselle. She was also nice and disarming. She gave me a drink, introduced me to Arthur, he welcomed me to the island. Then I started to feel dizzy. Last thing I remember she was coming at me with a needle and smiling. I wanted to kick her, but my legs were Jello. God, I was so helpless."

"Again. Not your fault."

"It felt incredible for a split second then I was in so much pain. All my training, my cop instincts were crap. I should've done something to stop it."

"You gotta stop beating yourself up over this. We all make mistakes. I probably shouldn't have chased Diablo."

"You didn't know he had cocaine in his pocket he was going to throw in your eyes. Is it better yet?"

"Still blurry, less burning."

"You should have your mom look at it."

"Nah. I'm okay."

Lying this close with her started out low-key, but now my dick is responding to the soft weight of her breasts pressing on me, the trusting look in her big brown eyes. The urge to fuck her comes back strong, and my hands move of their own will, caressing her back, feeling all the warm curves of her shoulders, waist, and hips. Her body is incredible, but she doesn't flaunt it. She keeps it covered in her demure clothes. Seeing her in that nightie was a rare treat. If she dressed like that all the time, I'd have trouble keeping my hands off her. Hard enough with her fully clothed.

Her shoulders hitch, and her forehead falls to my chest. Oh shit. She's crying. "Hey. It's all right. You're safe now."

"It's not that."

"What then?"

She looks up at me with tears in her eyes. "I'm sorry."

"For what?"

"For all the pain I caused you and your family. It was childish and spiteful. I forgave you, but can you ever forgive me?"

"I already have. You're forgiven."

She shakes her head. "There's more you don't know."

"I forgive you for that too."

"You don't even know what I did."

She tries to slide away, but my hand on her back pulls her face up close to mine.

"Doesn't matter. I forgive you. No grudges. We are who we are now. The past doesn't matter."

"And who are we now?"

"We're Mace and Loralei. It's that simple."

She bites her lip and looks down at mine. She's still blurry, but her breath brushes my cheek. She pushes up and plants a tentative, uneven kiss on my lips. I stay still and savor that. She wants me and she's going for it. It's gonna happen now, and nothing can stop us. I grab her ass and pull her up so she's straddling my dick.

An urgent knock at the door stops us both cold.

"Mace! You in there? Open up."

It's Remy. The heat drains from Lola's eyes, and she shuts down. She's off me in a hot second and running for the bathroom. I was so close to having her, and Remy ruined it all with a few bangs on my door.

I take a deep breath and try to calm my dick down. I can't answer the door with a raging boner. "One second."

"Open the door!" He bangs it again.

"Wait a hot fucking second, asshole." What the hell is his problem?

I take my time throwing on a shirt and walking to the door because I know it'll piss him off more.

When I open it, I shoot him a vicious glare. "What is your problem?"

"You bring that girl up here?" He stops and stares at my face. "What happened to your eye?"

"Long story."

He looks over my shoulder into my place. "Is Loralei here? Sutton saw you walking up with a girl."

"If she were here, would it be any of your business?"

"Are you shitting me? That girl is bad news. She's caused this family nothing but grief, and you bring her up here like she's not a pariah?"

Oh no. He's not going there. The lava in the volcano heats up and threatens to erupt. But this is my brother. I have to control it. "Yes, she's here, and she's terrified of exactly this, so chill out."

"I'm not scared." Loralei's voice draws both our attention behind us, where she's standing in the doorway to the bathroom.

Remy's nostril's flare. "What're you doing here?"

"I came here to help Mace with his eye, but if you're here, I guess I can leave."

"You're not leaving. She's not leaving." I make it clear in my tone there's no negotiating this.

"She's not staying. Not here." Remy walks inside. I'd have to fight him to stop him, so I let him pass. "She doesn't belong here. No old baggage from our pasts comes up the mountain, Mace. None."

"She's not old baggage from my past. I met her when I was twenty. I'd been living here for seven years already. She's new baggage." I step back and sit on the end of my bed.

"Hey!" Loralei crosses her arms and pops a hip.

"Either way, get her out before she causes more damage." He points to the door.

"She won't cause any damage. In case you forgot, she was kidnapped and held captive on Morganna's island. You rescued her. Where is all that now?"

"She looks fine now." His gaze scans her up and down.

"She lost her memory and just got it back. She could lose her job, and her kidnappers are still after her, so you think you can back the fuck off for fifteen minutes?"

He steps back and stares at her. "I didn't know all that."

"And you didn't take the time to ask either. So I'll repeat myself, and I don't like to do that. Back off."

Sutton steps into the cabin and stands next to Remy as she glares at Lola.

"You too, Sutton?"

"We all don't want her here."

"I'm fine with her here." My mom steps in next with my dad behind her. "If she needs help, we help her. We're not throwing her out on the street no matter what she did in the past."

Cutter and Cass walk in behind them, and my tiny cabin is suddenly crowded with Twists.

"What's going on?" my dad asks.

"This is Loralei Valentine. The girl we rescued from the island." Remy's voice is filled with disdain.

Cutter's gaze cuts to her. "And the one who started the fight with Jareth Quicksilver."

"And the one who revealed our location to Mom's relatives in New York," Remy adds.

Loralei steps back and her shoulders curl in. God, I hate that my family is making a huge deal out of this.

"And the one who lost her memory and just got it back and might be able to help you with Giselle." I remind Cutter that in the beginning he wanted Loralei to help him.

"You know where Giselle is?" Cutter asks her.

"No. I just know she was at the island, and she drugged me."

"That's better than nothing." Cutter steps back and throws an arm around Cass. "I say we let her stay if she helps us with Giselle."

"It's not up to you, Cutter or Remy or anybody. She's here with me, and you all need to get out of my cabin."

"What happened to your eye?" Cass asks me. She has a bandage on her arm, but otherwise looks okay after her ordeal on the island.

"Someone threw cocaine into it."

"Oh no."

My mom steps in and touches above my eye. "I should look at it. I might have something to put in there."

"It's fine. It's healing. Just blurry and red. So we need some time alone. Can we talk about this some other time when my eye isn't red, and Lola isn't going through the stress of getting her memory back?"

"She got her memory back? Oh, that's great." My mom is the only one who is happy. Everyone else acts cold and disinterested.

"Everyone out. We'll come to dinner tomorrow night." I usher them out the door.

Cass and Cutter nod and leave.

"Call me if you need anything," my mom calls as she walks out with my dad following.

Remy stays behind and keeps staring down Lola.

I have to hold back the urge to shove him out the door. "I don't know what your problem is, brother, but you need to get your eyes off her and back on your own business. She's not a threat right now, and you're crossing a line. Go take it out somewhere else, but she doesn't deserve your bullshit."

Sutton tugs at his arm. "It's all right, Remy. Let's go."

Remy turns his glare to me. "I'm doubting you, Mace. I'm doubting your loyalty to this family. She worth it? That toxic bitch worth turning your back on us?"

Loralei gasps and turns away. She closes the door to the bathroom behind her.

I stand up and get in his face. "Fuck you. Don't talk to her. Don't look at her, and never fucking doubt me."

His eyes flash and his jaw works, but he doesn't respond.

"Get out of my cabin. We'll see you at dinner." He's so lucky my eye is injured right now, or I'd take him down for that.

"Don't bring her to a family dinner." He throws out one last stupid jab.

I smash his shoulder and push him toward the door. "I'll bring whoever the hell I want." That's it. The Volcano is ready to blow, and he needs to run if he wants to live.

Remy stiffens but doesn't raise his fists. He steps back. He knows he's in the wrong, and he's pissing me off. He takes Sutton's hand and stomps out.

In his wake, he leaves an awkward silence between me and a shell-shocked Loralei, who has opened the door to see if the coast is clear.

"Hold me back because I'm about to beat the crap out of my brother."

"No. Don't do that. Calm down, Volcano." She walks to me and touches my forearm. It helps take the edge off, but I'm still about to blow.

"Get me out of here. Seriously. Let's go somewhere, so I don't track him down and make him eat his tonsils."

"Oh my God. Okay. Let's go."

On the walk to her car, I'm scanning every inch of the place for Remy. I want to beat his brains in for what he said.

"Where to?"

"Anywhere."

She starts the car and drives out of the lot, saving my brother's life.

Chapter 10 Hot Sauce

Loralei

"Hamburgers, deli food, or Mexican." The small town of Boulder Creek only has three restaurants that I can see.

On the ride here, we didn't talk. He messed with my radio stations, tapped his foot, and stared out the side window. I absolutely understand why they call him Volcano. Hot magma bubbles inside him, and he could spew it out over an entire city at any moment.

"Mexican. It's the only place with booze."

I pull into Javier's Cantina, and Mace meets me in front of the car. He's not huffing and puffing anymore, but the veins in his neck are still prominent, and he's still checking over his shoulder like someone is going to jump him.

He opens the door for me, the hostess looks up, and her eyes widen before a flirty grin appears on her lips. "Hey, Mace." She rocks side to side trying to get his attention, but he's deep in his mood and just grunts at her. "Why don't you sit over here?"

We follow her to a booth and settle in opposite each other. He picks up the hot sauce bottle, reads the label, and sets it down. He's like a caged animal, and I'm starting to think I should've taken him someplace where he could run wild and kill bunnies instead of cramming him into this tiny booth and forcing him to sit still.

A waitress brings us tortilla chips with salsa and asks what we want to drink.

He dives into the chips before she even stops speaking. "Roca Patron Silver. Bottle and two shot glasses."

When he looks up, the waitress stares a little too long at his eye and her smile fades. "Sure."

He sprinkles salt on the chips and shovels huge scoops of salsa into his mouth.

The waitress returns with a bottle of tequila, a plate of limes, and two shot glasses. He pours two shots and downs his with no preamble. He realizes I haven't moved and finally makes eye contact with me. "Drink."

"No thanks."

"You ordered a whiskey sour last night."

"I'm driving tonight."

He shoves another chip in his mouth. "You need to lose control more often. It's piping hot. Like hot sauce." He picks up the bottle of hot sauce and shakes it. "Muy caliente."

I chuckle at him. "Whatever you say." I'm glad he's cheering up and cracking jokes again.

"I'm telling you. Inner lioness is bored shitless with your control issues and wants to roam free. Drink tequila. Fuck on the hood of her Maserati. Let her have some fun."

"Um." The truth is I have envisioned having sex with Mace in my car many times—not really on the hood—but only in private fantasies. It's never something I'd really do. "I'll send her a memo that Mace thinks she needs to come out and play more often." And tell her to get more creative with my fantasies. Why did I not think of the hood of the car?

The waitress brings our food, and he leans back to allow her to place a steaming plate of fajitas in front of him. She hands me a chicken tostada bowl that smells divine. "Anything else?"

"No. We're fine. Thank you."

The food entrances him. He takes his time assembling a tortilla with steak and peppers, carefully adding drops of hot sauce and sour cream. I have to smile at him. He's full speed ahead on chips and salsa, but when fajitas show up, he's on the slow boat to happy town.

"You ready to talk?" I finally ask him in a low voice.

His eyes scan the restaurant before landing on me. "Getting there."

"This is why I didn't want to go to your family's place. I don't want to come between you guys." I speak quietly because there's ears everywhere in a small town.

He bites into his fajita burrito and chews as he stares down at his plate. "Remy was out of line."

"Not really. I did all those things and more." If he knew what the more was, he wouldn't keep offering me such blanket forgiveness. He'd be furious with me and send me packing.

"I don't give a shit. If I bring you home, I'm vouching for you. He needs to accept it or face my fists."

"I really don't think fighting is going to help." I hate the idea of Remy and Mace fighting over me. They're brothers. They should love each other and not let a girl come between them.

"A good grudge match helps everything." He grins, and I'm caught off guard again by his smile. With his eye red and his mouth full, he looks extra dangerous, and it's sexy in a twisted way.

"It's not necessary for them to accept me. Why force it?"

He looks into my eyes. "We're going after Diablo. I need their help."

"*We* are not going after Diablo. I'll handle it myself."

"We've already determined this is way too dangerous for you on your own."

"Then I'll get the department involved. I'm not dragging you into this."

He raises his arms to the side, palms up, looking down at himself. "Already dragged, babe."

I see his point. He is in this pretty deep with me. "You mentioned Giselle to Cutter. Is that what this is about?"

"Part of it."

"What's the other part?"

"You." He shoves the last of his first fajita in his mouth and grins.

"Me?"

"I like you. This is fun." He picks up his next tortilla and starts the slow process of preparing another one.

Watching Mace eat is so fascinating, I haven't even touched my food. "You think I'm fun?"

"You could be more fun if you'd lighten up, but yeah, I enjoy your company."

"Wow. I'm shocked." I take a bite of my chicken tostada. The salsa is mildly spicy, and the lettuce is fresh. It's good.

He shrugs. "Me too."

"So what? You're like my partner now?"

"If that's what you wanna call it."

"That won't work."

"It's working so far. And I really want to fuck you."

"Oh my God, Mace. Do you have no filters at all?"

"It's no secret. I like your inner lioness. She likes me. We're gonna get it on and make some noise."

"I'm never going to sleep with you again."

He downs another shot of tequila. "Tomorrow we're going on a hike."

"I don't have time. I need to do tons of research on Diablo. His connections to my dad. I have an idea to hack into his phone."

He shakes his head. "We're going on a hike to Hopper's Ledge."

"Uh. I'm actually afraid of heights, especially places that end in the word *ledge*."

"Trust. Our problem is you don't trust me, and I don't trust you. We need to work it out in nature. On the ledge." He downs another shot, hissing after he gulps it down his throat.

"So this is how you solve problems? Beat your brother into submission and push me off a ledge?"

"I wouldn't word it that way, but essentially, yes."

"It won't work." I shake my head and take another bite of my food. He's being irrational and random.

"You'll see. My brother will back you up, and I'll be parking my truck in your garage of love in a few days."

My stomach does a little flip at his certainty, and my inner lioness growls and claws at her cage. "Never gonna happen."

We finish up our meal, and he pays after downing two more shots. He doesn't seem drunk but his step is lighter, eyes lazy. He's back to his casual self.

"Night, Mace." The hostess tries one last time to get his attention. He ignores her and grabs my hand. I have to admit it's satisfying in a juvenile way.

At the car, he tugs me over to the front bumper and pulls a quick move that lands me on my back on the hood. He falls forward on top of me and laughs, the trace scent of the tequila warming my nose. "Think of it. How good it would be. Your pants down, legs wrapped behind my back, my dick sliding in and out of your tight pussy." He bends down to give me a sensual spicy tequila kiss.

His deep voice and salacious words light up my body. Unbearable heat and strength press into me as I caress his massive shoulders. My inner lioness begs me to have sex with him right here. No way. I can't do that. I give her a minute to enjoy it. I feel hot where he touches me like a live wire about to ignite, but he's gotten too cocky. He's taken for granted he can push me on top of my car, and I'll submit.

I reach down and undo his jeans. His huge dick bursting out the top makes me gasp for air. It's a behemoth of a creature. We could have so much fun with that. But instead, I get my hands around it, grab hard, twist, and pull.

His head flies back and he groans.

"Never forget I'm a cop. I know how to protect myself."

His head comes back down, and his grimace transforms into a smile. "You think I didn't like that? Do it again."

I growl and let go. "No. Get off me."

He's still grinning as he backs off and starts buttoning his jeans. He makes a snarling sound like a hungry grizzly bear.

Oh my God. I've met my match with Mace. What am I gonna do with him? I have to admit I'm enjoying his company too. I'm still in awe of his giant cock and how he loved when I roughed him up. I don't know if rock climbing or fighting with Remy will solve any of our problems, but it's going to be an adventure either way.

Chapter 11 Hopper's Ledge

Mace went straight to bed when we got back to his cabin. I sighed and let the exhaustion of the day take me too as I lay down next to him.

I wake up curled like a pretzel in his arms. It feels good so I don't move for a while. I allow myself a moment to imagine how awesome it would be if Mace was my man and we were in love waking up like this.

Is there any way we could actually do that? He's so different from me, his family hates me, he's hurt me before. There's just too many roadblocks, and yet a secret part of my heart wishes my inner lioness could come out to play permanently and ride along with Mace on his magical mystery world of carefree fun. I'd have to abandon all the promises I made in my dad's memory, and I'm not sure I'm ready to do that yet.

So I wiggle my arm and try to break free. He reflexively squeezes me tighter, and his lips come down to land on my temple as he hums low and deep. Why does he have to be so dreamy? It's almost impossible to resist him like this. Every fiber of my being yearns to turn to him, kiss him, and make love with him. I have to call on years of discipline to force him away.

"I need to work on Diablo. I have a plan to get data from his phone, but it's gonna take a lot of work."

"Surf's up. Let's go."

"Surfing? I thought you wanted to hike to a ledge?"

"After," he mumbles without opening his eyes.

"No. I'm working today." I can't follow along with his whims. This is serious.

His arm squeezes me tighter, and he fully opens his eyes. "Breakfast then hike. Surfing another time."

I sigh and tap at his arm. "You'll have to let me go if we're going to do those things."

He grumbles and lifts his arm, giving me a chance to sneak out of his warm clutches.

I run to the bathroom and wash my face. Today is going to be a challenge. One thing about Mace, he has my mind spinning so fast, I haven't had time to dwell on my returned memories. I'm sure it will hit me at some point, but right now it's all about Mace.

Thinking of him reminds me I forgot to ask about his eye. "How's your eye?" I peek out of the bathroom and see his gorgeous body still sprawled out on the bed, one knee bent, arms up behind his head. He's all tan skin and muscles. A true Hawaiian Jesus with his hair spilled on the pillow like a crown of thorns. The sheet covering his private parts is like a shroud around the mystery of life.

"It's okay." He rubs his eyes and sits up in the bed.

I turn my attention back to the bathroom and attempt to focus on getting ready. He walks in behind me and leans down to look in the mirror. The red has faded to a light pink. "It looks better."

"Yep. I'll survive another day," he says casually.

"You could've lost your vision."

"But I didn't. You want breakfast? I make a killer pancake."

"Wow. I'm surprised. Okay. Knock yourself out."

"You wanna?" He tilts his head toward the toilet.

"Oh, sorry." My gaze darts to his shorts and away again. Mace is all man, and it's undeniably obvious when he's walking around in his underwear.

I leave the bathroom and grab my laptop. Mace has a chair and side table set up next to his fireplace, and that'll work fine as a workspace for me until we leave for the hike.

Thirty minutes later, Mace has thankfully put on some clothes, and I've managed to get started on collecting Diablo's private info so I can answer his security questions and get his phone transferred over to a burner.

Mace sets two plates with large, thin pancakes on a small kitchen table with benches built into the wall. "Those look more like crepes than pancakes."

"You could call 'em crepes if you want to. Just don't tell anyone I made you crepes." He winks and grins.

I laugh and take a seat. "Secret's safe with me. If anyone asks, I'll tell them Mace made me a huge stack of thick, fluffy pancakes."

He adds powdered sugar, syrup, and frozen fruit to the table as toppings. "Maybe it's best we just keep the whole cooking thing between us."

"All right." I scoop some fruit onto my crepe. He did a good job too. Not burned, evenly cooked. "I like to cook too."

He smothers his pancake in syrup and butter. "What kind of food?"

"I like to try things from all around the world. Italy, Spain, Thailand, Greece."

He nods and cuts into his pancake that's really a crepe. "How'd you learn that?"

"Well, mostly I traveled with my father and took notes then tried it myself. Once we took a slow boat from Thailand to Laos. We had these lemongrass rice noodles with vegetables. Every time I make that dish, I remember how my father and I cuddled in the chilly morning air on the boat."

Oops. I brought up my dad again. He's quiet and looks down. Last night he jokingly mentioned that I promised to forgive him, but we didn't really talk about it.

"I miss him, Mace, but I don't blame you for his death anymore. I forgive you. I understand why you arrested him. I still don't think you needed to seduce me to do it, but the other part I forgive."

He winces and nods. When he looks up at me, the heat in his eyes steals my breath. "I didn't have to seduce you. Your dad would've been easy enough to catch. I wanted to touch the blue sky, so I did it." His deep voice rumbles and sends a zing down my spine. Mace keeps giving me these signs that he likes me, and it's getting harder to resist.

"Okay then." I brush my hands together like I'm wiping off bread crumbs, even though we just had crepes. "Shall we go on a hike so you can push me off a ledge?"

He chuckles and stands to clear the table. "Yeah. Get ready."

***

We drive in an old Jeep up to a trailhead. Mace is less fidgety today, and he seems comfortable on these roads. "I take it you've hiked this trail before?"

"Only a thousand times. My brothers and I basically grew up here."

"But I thought you were adopted when you were a teenager."

"I was. But I became a man here."

"Ahh." If there is any place to become a man, it's here among these towering coastal redwoods that have survived so many challenges. Storms, fires, droughts, lightning, logging. Hundreds of years and here they stand.

We park in the one space marked by a log. As he's pulling the gear from the Jeep, I check the place out. Water rushes in the background, lots of critters peeping and chirping. The air is incredibly fresh and smells like pine. The sign has a lot of warnings, but the biggest one is danger of falling from rocks, and there's a picture of a stick figure plummeting into the abyss.

"Let's go." He's wearing shorts with big pockets and a tattered white T-shirt that looks well-loved and worn. He throws a small pack over his shoulders and walks toward the trailhead with confidence in his step.

The path isn't steep, and it's fully shaded by redwoods. Ferns and sorrel bushes make a pretty understory in the decaying leaf litter from the trees.

After about five minutes on the slowly ascending trail, I'm settling into the relaxation only nature can bring. Mace seems more tranquil too. "So tell me one secret no one else knows about you," he asks over his shoulder.

"Oh. Hmm. Well. I've never been to Disneyland."

"That's a shame. Star Wars Land is the bomb."

Now he has me wondering why my dad didn't take me. "The life of a celebrity's daughter is different. You don't just wake up and decide to go to Disneyland that day. You have to make arrangements. It's just not something we ever did." We could have gone. What was his excuse? He's not here for me to ask anymore, so I'll never know.

"Mmm."

I can hear Mace judging my dad and not buying my excuses. "Tell me something about you no one else knows," I throw back at him.

"My bio father was a deadbeat dad who got arrested by a bounty hunter."

My step falters, and I'm staring at the back of his head. "Are you kidding me?"

He doesn't break his stride or look back. "Nope. The bounty hunter was named Wayne. He's a bail bondsman now. Still work with him."

So Mace went through what I did? He knows how it feels to have your family ripped apart? "Tell me more."

"I was in Hawaii. My dad left us. My mom couldn't work, had mental problems. Wayne arrested him, and I ended up in foster care in Georgia. That sucked."

All these years I've known and hated Mace, I never knew how he ended up being a Twist or where he came from. I expected to hear Hawaii, but not Georgia. "What happened there?"

"I didn't fit in. Bounced around group homes. Ended up with a religious family that didn't like the way I was. Sent me to a boarding school to retrain me. Assholes there tied my wrists to try to get me to stop moving. Got the hell out of there and ran away to California. Met Cutter, Sutton, and Remy. We all got lucky and got adopted by Foster and Mila."

I catch up to him and take his hand. "Oh my gosh. I swear I didn't know any of that."

He twines his fingers in mine and pulls me forward to walk side-by-side with him. "How would you know? And does it change anything?"

"Yes. It does because I see now why you might've become a bounty hunter yourself. You go after deadbeat dads?"

"Mostly. Exceptions for assholes that hurt women." He shrugs. "Tell me another secret."

I take a moment to collect my thoughts and listen to the sounds of the forest. "I only hated you because I liked you so much. I was obsessed with you and jealous. Hated that I couldn't be like you."

He stops and stares down at me with his cobalt blue eyes that look so stunning against the forest canopy. He hasn't shaved and a scruffy shadow covers his sexy jaw. His tentative grin spreads into a full-blown smile that creates attractive wrinkles around his eyes. "My turn. I never hated you. Was always intrigued by you. When I followed you, it wasn't because you were a threat. I wanted a glimpse into your life."

My tummy flips. "And what did you see?"

He looks up into the trees before answering. "I saw the beautiful girl I knew had grown up to be a gorgeous lioness, but she was lonely. She needed someone to protect her. I stepped in to make that happen, and when I did, it felt right." He shrugs like it's not a big deal, but it means everything to me.

Mace is blowing my mind with this talk. It's hard to believe him, but there's no stiffness in his shoulders, nothing in his eyes tells me he's lying.

The tree canopy opens up, and we're staring at a towering peak with big boulders at the base. He hops up and offers me a hand. "This is the fun part."

MEMORIZING MACE

As we climb, the rocks get steeper and narrower, and I have to watch my step as I battle the fear of heights that threatens to ruin this awesome day. We're high above a ravine now, and one mis-step could be deadly. Whenever the path gets really narrow, Mace turns back to watch me and gives me a hand when I need it.

We come across a huge rock plateau, and my stomach pitches when I look down at the valley below. "I take it this is Hopper's Ledge?"

"This is the hopping part. The ledge is up there."

He steps out to the edge and jumps across the gap. My heart lurches up into my throat.

"Mace!"

"I've done this jump a thousand times. Now, you." He holds out his hand.

The gap is about five feet wide, but it's not the width that scares me. It's the depth. We're at least five hundred feet up with nothing but rocks and trees below. I feel like I'm the stick figure about to fall into the abyss. "I can't."

"Yes, you can. I've got you."

"This is crazy."

"You don't have to jump. There's another way around. This one is more fun."

This does not feel like fun, but he's challenged me, and I'm not giving up.

"Think of how good it's gonna feel when you make it. You can sail over that thing. Stop worrying."

My gosh. Mace is actually convincing me to jump off a cliff. And the insane part is I'm thinking of doing it.

"If I die..."

"You won't."

"If I do, I support my three half-siblings. They get everything I have. It's not much, but..."

He freezes for a second. "You support them?"

"Yes! If I die, they won't have anyone. Please, send them all my money."

He bites his bottom lip and nods his head. "Can I have the Maserati?"

"Mace!"

"Fine. The kids get the car too."

"Can we stop talking about this?"

"If you would jump, we could."

I take a deep breath. Okay. I can do this. I've been in dangerous situations before. I just need to call on my inner Charlie's Angels detective skills. What if I was chasing a perp and had to jump? I'd do it no problem. My father had me walking on coals every weekend at his retreats. It's all about conquering the fear and pushing through.

I close my eyes, bend my knees, and imagine myself flying over the gap.

"That's good." He's smiling on the other side, his big arms spread out to catch me. Can I trust him? What if he really did plan all this to get me out here to kill me?

No, the smile on his lips is too innocent for that. I trust him.

I swing my arms out and launch myself in his direction. My face plows into the fabric of Mace's shirt, and there's a terrifying moment where I'm tumbling down. His strong arms wrap around my back, and he breaks our fall as we hit the granite together. "Overkill, babe."

I'm laughing and looking down at his gleaming smile. "I did it."

"You were awesome." His eyes sparkle, and his hands rub up and down my back. Not in a friendly way. In a sensual way that tells me he's clearly checking out my curves.

I lean down and plant a hard kiss on his lips. His mouth opens and our tongues tangle in a hot, wet, out-in-nature kiss. I end it to proclaim, "I conquered the ledge. I can't believe it."

His gaze sweeps up to the steep rocks next to us. "Nope. That's next."

"Oh my Lord, save me."

He pops up and offers me a hand. "You can do it. I believe in you."

I don't know where Mace gets all this faith in me, but I'll take it and use it for motivation. We climb to the base of a huge exposed granite face. At the top, a thick ledge cantilevers out from the formation.

"Is that the ledge?"

"Yep."

"And we're going to climb it?"

"Yep." He's way too happy about the fear on my face.

"I'm not climbing that."

"There's a rope." He points to an old worn rope anchored into the rock.

"Just a rope on the rock? That's going to keep us from falling?"

"It's safe. People hike this rock all the time. Follow me."

He takes off up the rock without missing a step. I'm frozen to the spot. The thought of falling has me paralyzed.

"You comin'?"

I shake my head. "Not this time."

He rolls his eyes and hops back down to me. "Like this." He stands behind me and wraps his hot, warm body around my limbs. He folds us forward and places my hands on the rope, forcing me to take hold and accept we're doing this. "Good. Now one step." His foot pushes on mine and somehow I manage to do it. It's so steep we're almost standing up but we're bent over enough I can feel every inch of him moving against my skin. The scruff on his chin and his hot breath caress my ear. "If you fall, I fall."

The confident rumble in his voice is exactly what I need to relax. Suddenly the fear is gone, and my thoughts zero in on Mace's thighs rubbing the back of my legs, his hips against my butt, his long arms resting over mine, his breath wisping by my ear. He has me caged in a giant bear hug that warms my soul and eases my insurmountable fears.

As we climb, more of the breathtaking tree tops in the valley come into view. Crisp fresh air fills my lungs and exultant freedom washes over me. I feel like I could sing. What was I worried about before? Mace made this so fun and so worth it.

Mace's focus has narrowed in on me, and his intensity is hitting me full blast, making my knees weak and my tummy flip. Normally I would stop him when he gets this close, but I can't bring myself to say it. "This feels different."

"Mmm." His lips slide across my neck as we reach a flatter area close to the peak of the rock. He presses his fully hard cock against my back and I gasp.

"The view is fantastic." I move to stand up fully but he keeps his strong frame wrapped around me so I'm bent forward.

"Uh-huh." Mace opens his mouth on my neck and sucks hard. It sends shivers through my spine. His hands, now free of the ropes, move to my belly and press flat. His hips slide down and press me to the hard granite that is still warm from the day's sun. He undulates his hips against my butt and I'm gone. I have no willpower to fight him off. I want this as bad as he does, and I'm not dumb enough to keep saying no. When am I ever going to get another chance to make out with Mace on top of a mountain like this?

I twist my head, and he plants a kiss on my lips over my shoulder. His entire body presses me into the rock, his hard dick sliding between my butt cheeks and making me hungry for him. He removes his hands from my stomach and massages down my legs, up my arms, and into my hair. "I'm gonna take you right here," he whispers in my ear. "Make you come so hard you'll never forget."

A whimper is all I can manage back. I'm pretty sure he can have anything he wants right now, and I'll remember it forever. I raise my hips and push against his hard cock. He presses back and pins me to the rock. He keeps me like that for a long time, just kissing my lips, my neck and upper back. It's torture being face down because I can't reach him or truly kiss him back with my head at this angle. I'm forced to relax and enjoy it, so that's what I do.

He hums with pleasure as his wet tongue traces every inch of my neck. Finally, he raises his torso slightly and turns me to my back. He dives in and his mouth kisses all the parts he couldn't reach when I was on my stomach. My hands are free to grab him now.

Our kisses are greedy like we want to gobble down the first few bites of a delicious meal. His thick curly hair twines between my fingers. I've wanted to get my hands on it for so long, and now I have free rein to touch it. My other hand snakes down to grab his butt which is round and firm. His perfection that taunted me all these years is within my grasp and mine to enjoy. I can't believe he's as eager for me as I am for him.

His hard cock presses against my leg through the fabric of our shorts. We're not going to take off our clothes out here. Are we?

He reaches for my shirt and tugs it out of my shorts. Looks like we are getting naked. I'm not stopping him.

He grunts and works the buttons open while I'm pushing his shorts lower on his ass. My fingers explore his tempting butt dimples. Amazing. I've lost all my fears of privacy or someone seeing us. This is too urgent to care about things like that.

He gets my shirt open and continues kissing me from my neck down to the curves of my breasts. He kisses down my belly and works my shorts open. This is all happening so fast, but I want it. I couldn't stop him if I wanted to. This train has left the station and has no brakes.

I'm struck by a delicious mix of cool air and the heat from his lips caressing my skin as he yanks my bottoms down. He lowers his head, laving his tongue from back to front before dipping it deep, drawing a raspy hiss from the back of my throat. His mouth, tongue, and hands all work together in harmony and steal my breath. It doesn't take long before my stomach clenches and a thunderous pressure builds between my legs. "Oh. Oh my God." My orgasm crashes through me like a giant earthquake, the initial shock and lingering pulses shaking my entire body. My cry echoes into the canyon below.

He groans and continues to dine on my lower half. I grab his hair and pull him up. He's grinning like a mad man with shining lips and messed up hair. "So good. So sweet. Like honey. You're goddamn beautiful." He lowers his head to kiss me, and I taste myself on his lips. "I'm taking you up to the ledge."

Deep in my brain, I know I should be afraid, but I seriously trust Mace to take care of me. He scoops me up, and I wrap my legs around his waist as we clomp up the last bit of slope to the top of the ledge. We don't bother to take in the view. We're too busy ripping each other's clothes off.

I reach down and grab his dick and do the twist and pull he liked before. "You like that?"

"Love it." He grits his teeth and closes his eyes.

My hand works his huge shaft, and I love watching the pleasure on his face.

"Not waiting anymore. Taking you now." Mace surges up and positions himself between my legs. After a moment of lining up, he pushes in and groans.

He works his hips up and down until he's fully seated inside me, and I'm stretched full of Mace. Then the magic begins. He grinds his hips, rubbing our bodies together, filling me deeper and harder and smashing my clit with each thrust. It's everything I thought it would be, and I want it to last forever.

Mace is kissing me again, one elbow braced on the rock over my head, the other hand reaching down to tilt my hips toward him, getting impossibly closer and deeper.

I dig my nails into the pistoning muscles of his shoulders and lock my ankles behind his back. Every stroke is like heaven.

We go at it like that for a while, getting to know each other's bodies and how we move. It's never been like this before. The last time with Mace wasn't this good. It never got close to this with Griffin. Mace is magnificent.

I feel it rising from my spine. "I'm coming again."

"Yes. Come on my dick. So good." His back arches, he grunts and freezes as he buries himself deep and we fall over the edge together. We're planted solid on the rock, but inside we're freefalling to the valley below.

He thrusts slower, and he's kissing me again as he pumps in and out. "I knew it. I knew we'd be incredible together again."

"Mmm."

"This side of you I'll never get enough of. Want it all the time. It's so pure and totally honest about who you are."

"I like this side of you too." I smack his bare ass.

He grins and collapses on top of me with his chin against my neck. We lay like that in the afternoon sun, catching our breath and basking in the glory of what we shared.

His head rises, and he looks around with hooded lids. We've both been so unaware of our surroundings, we didn't hear the helicopter coming.

But there it is, directly above us, a large helicopter hovers and blows strong wind down on us. "Get the fuck out of here!" Mace screams.

"You know who that is?"

"It's Remy."

Remy? Oh my God, Remy. I push him off but he won't budge. "Don't get up. He'll see you naked. Probably taking pictures up there."

"Oh my God." I tuck my forehead into his chest. Remy is taking pictures of us naked, doing it on a rock.

Mace reaches back and flips off the helicopter. "Fuck you, Remy!"

Finally, the helicopter gains altitude and flies away.

"That asshole. I'll kill him."

"No brother killing over me."

"No. But I'm gonna pummel him so hard." He kisses me one more time before pulling out. He grabs a towel from his backpack and tenderly wipes between my legs. "I can't believe he did that."

I stay quiet and stare at Mace's strong arms reverently working between my legs. He hands me my clothes and starts to dress.

"How did he even know we were here?" I ask him.

"I have a few favorite spots. He probably was out looking for me." He finishes dressing and pulls me into his arms. "Ignore him. You were awesome."

I have to smile. "You were pretty impressive yourself."

"I didn't use a..."

"I'm on the pill, but yeah, maybe next time we should." I wink at him.

"Next time might be in five minutes." His arms squeeze tight around me.

"It will not."

He glances up to the sky. "Okay. Let's go home first. Twenty minutes until next time."

That makes me laugh. "Okay."

Chapter 12 Sunday Dinner

Mace

"I'm going to beat his ass." Remy's helicopter finally leaves, and I'm alone with Loralei again. She looked so gorgeous after she came. Her face and body relaxed, and she was totally open to me. A man would give his life's savings to have a woman look at him like she looked at me. It was as memorable as I thought it would be. Better because she loved it so much. Better because of the rock and the view and mostly because she totally lost control and yelled my name into the basin.

She was giving in to this. She was letting me claim her.

I help her get dressed, and we share more kisses before starting down Hopper's Ledge. I'm not usually a kissy kinda guy, but Loralei's lips are the exception. I'd stay lip-locked with her for days if I didn't have to eat. And that's my plan. Eat and hook up with her again.

"Thank you, Mace."

I don't know what she's thanking me for but her eyes are lazy, her hair messed up, and her lips curled up in a permagrin. I'm thinking it's the two orgasms I gave her causing her to look like that, but I don't care. I love this side of Loralei, and I'll do everything I can to bring it out of her.

I follow her on the way down. She seems a lot more confident. She's still smiling when we hit the flatter part of the trail. "We're going to dinner tonight." I throw an arm over her shoulder, and she tenses.

"I don't think I'm welcome there."

"Of course you are."

I don't like the way she's pulling away from me and hiding in her shell again. "I want you there. If anyone has a problem with it, they can talk to me. Most of them are cool with it. Remy and Sutton overreacted."

She flinches when I say Remy and Sutton.

"C'mon. You're a cop. You can't take a little sass from my sister and assholery from my brother? Stand strong, and they'll respect you like I do."

"You respect me now?"

I stop her and force her to look into my eyes. "More than respect. I'm digging you now." We start walking again.

"Why?"

I take her hand in mine and give it a squeeze. "I don't know. Maybe it's the way you woke up in a hospital with huge portions of your memory missing and still had the wherewithal to put me in my place. Thought that was fun."

"It wasn't fun. It was fight or flight."

"Then you rocked the outfit at the club you were totally not comfortable with and made it work out with Helix. Nice job."

"That was easy."

"It wouldn't be for a lot of women."

She shrugs and I throw an arm over her shoulder. "Then you did an awesome job facing down Diablo. He's a scary dude. Now, you should've gone the wrong way down that street, but other than that you were badass."

"Shut up." She smacks me in the gut.

"I like the way you faced your fear of heights, and I especially like tasting your sweet nectar out here on the ledge." I lean down and kiss her ear. She raises her shoulder and laughs like it tickles. "I can see you try to keep control of things, but you let go for me. I find your brand of orderly on the outside, reluctant vixen on the inside incredibly appealing. It's like a secret you only share with me."

"That's bizarre."

"Don't you find my brand of crazy appealing?"

"No." She's fighting back laughter.

"You sure?"

She stops walking and turns toward me, one hand on my stomach, the other on my back. "All right. Yes. I absolutely love your brand of crazy. Sex on a cliff, running full speed without a plan, long hair flying wild, stylish clothes and don't-give-a-shit attitude."

"Is that all you like about me?" I raise my hand to caress her cheek with my palm.

"I admit I was touched when you offered to help me remember, and I'm very grateful that you rescued me from the island."

"Mmm. Anything else?" I run my thumb over her lower lip.

"I really love your hard-as-rock abs and your massive cock." She pats my abs and grins.

"Excellent." I nod and take her hand again. Today was epic. Loralei Valentine and me are an awesome pair. Just need to convince my family of this.

***

We walk into my parents' cabin thirty minutes late for dinner. Everyone glances at us and goes back to what they were doing. "See? No problem."

She's smiling and looking around the room, but I can see the tension in her jaw.

My mom approaches first, but two kids and a dog beat her to it. Maisey and Henry wrap their little arms around my legs as the dog jumps up to my chest.

I lift one of the tooth necklaces over my head and wiggle it over Maisey's mass of curly hair. She breaks into a squeal and a jump that makes me bonk her in the nose. "Hold on." She keeps bouncing as I finally work it over her head. The child is as wiggly as I was at her age. Still am. We're kindred spirits.

Maisey picks up the tooth and stares at it with wide eyes. "Did you kill someone to get this?"

"No. It's a coyote tooth, and he was already dead. I just took it for you because I thought it was cool for a necklace."

"It is. I love it."

Henry has been waiting patiently. "You want one too?"

He nods and I pull another one from my neck. "Don't let anyone tell you boys can't wear necklaces. This looks like a shark's tooth and all your friends are gonna think you wrestled a shark to get it."

"Thanks, Mace." He and Maisey run away, jump over the couch in the living room, and start wrestling.

My mom tugs the dog away and gives me a bear hug. I embrace her tiny frame in my arms. "Your eye better?" She squints up at me.

"All better, Ma."

"Good. I'll take this." She reaches for the serving dish Lola has been holding in her hands. "You didn't have to bring anything."

"Mace said it's potluck, and with the holidays coming up, I thought yams might be appropriate."

My mom's face lights up. "Yams? Did you make them from scratch?"

"Well, yeah. It's..."

My mom breaks out into laughter with her head thrown back. Lola smiles politely through the whole outburst.

"That's great. It's time we ate some homemade yams again." She flashes me a smile and walks back into the kitchen with the dish. I place my hand on the small of Lola's back to encourage her to walk into the room.

"What was that about?" She steps back like she's ready to run out the door.

I lean down and speak in her ear. "My mom screwed up some yams a while ago, and we haven't had them since."

"I didn't realize it was an issue. Why didn't you tell me?"

"I forgot until she started laughing. Now I remember the burnt marshmallows and the lumpy orange potatoes. It was bad." I stick out my tongue and she grimaces. "It's okay. It'll be fine. Let's go."

I give her a stronger push on the lower back, and she shuffles forward. Everyone is either watching TV or talking in the kitchen. They haven't sat down to dinner yet. We always start late. As we walk deeper into the room, Cutter and Cass look up from a movie on TV and give us a nod. My dad walks up and shares the Twist handshake, drawing out the hug part to say hello again and welcome me back to Sunday dinner. It's been at least a month since I showed up to one.

"How're you guys doing?" He's mostly looking at me, but it's nice he included Lola.

"We're good. Went climbing at Hopper's Ledge today."

He nods. "Clears the mind."

"Ah, yeah." We cleared a lot of things up there, but I'm not telling my dad, and it looks like Remy didn't rat me out either. "Remy here?"

"In the kitchen."

Lola's back stiffens, and I rub it to reassure her. Remy is the most decent of my brothers. She doesn't have to fear him. "I'm gonna introduce her to everyone else."

My dad nods and heads to the kitchen.

I introduce her to Blaine first. "This is Loralei."

His head twists and he does a double take. "The Loralei? Like glitter dildos Loralei?"

"You know about that?'

"Of course, it's legend. Nice to meet you, Loralei." He gives her a fist bump which she stiffly returns. I don't know what else Blaine knows about her, and I'm not sticking around to tell him.

I introduce her to Marshawn and Sequoia. If they know about the dildos, they are nice enough not to mention it. I have to keep rubbing her shoulders to get them down. "It's just my family. Don't stress."

She nods as Remy comes out of the kitchen carrying her dish. He stops when he sees her before finishing up and putting it on the table. He lifts the lid and sees the perfectly toasted marshmallows on top. "What the hell is that?"

"It's yams," I answer.

"I know what it is. Who brought it?"

Lola raises her hand and smiles. "Me."

Remy's gaze narrows in on her and he points. "You brought yams to our family dinner?" His tone implies she brought monkey brains.

"Shut up, Remy. It's just fucking sweet potatoes." I'm not allowing him to give her any more grief.

"We don't eat that shit at our house." The lid makes a cracking sound when he slams it back on the yams.

He is pissing me off, attacking her like this. "There's no manifesto on the door saying yams are forever banned. We just haven't had them. Tonight we do."

My mom comes out of the kitchen with another dish. "What's going on?"

"Remy's giving Lola a hard time for bringing yams."

He scowls at me for ratting him out to my mom, but I know she's on my side on this one. She's thrilled about the yams and she likes Loralei. "Not everyone likes them, but some people do. I'm sure they're better than the fiasco my yams were. Take a seat."

Sutton comes out and places some food on the table before taking a seat next to Remy. "Are those yams?"

I groan and take Lola's hand. "They are fucking yams! It's Thanksgiving in a week. Everyone chill."

Sutton and Remy share a look like they both think yams are a felony worthy of burning Lola at the stake.

The dishes start to move around as we all fork stuff onto our plates. Maisey plops down next to me and taps her plastic cup on the table. "Can I have juice?"

"No," my mom answers. "Just have water with dinner."

I don't blame my mom. Maisey is amped up without juice. With juice, she'll be a Tasmanian devil.

"I want to try the fucking yams," Maisey blurts out and we all stare at her.

"Maisey," my dad cautions her.

"What? That's what Mace called them."

My dad looks at me like *what did you do*?

"No cussing, Maisey." I wag my finger at her.

She smirks because she knows she can cuss with me when her parents aren't listening. She can even get away with it in front of them sometimes.

The other usual suspects at a Twist dinner make their way around the table. Pizza, Chinese egg rolls, Sutton's salad packed with veggies. The bright orange sweet potatoes with roasted marshmallows dripping off the top stand out on the plates as the only holiday food.

Remy and Sutton pass on the yams and start eating.

Lola keeps her head down, and I have to pat her knee under the table to get her to look at me. "Hey."

"It's fine. I'm fine."

She doesn't look fine, but she's holding it in.

"The yams are incredible," my mom says with a smile.

Lola nods but doesn't look up again.

"I love them," Maisey screams. "Give some to Henry. Do you like them? Who else loves them?" she asks the entire table.

I hear mumbles of "delicious," but Remy and Sutton keep quiet with jaws locked and hard eyes directing arrows at Lola. I feel like jumping in front of her and taking every dirty look they're giving her in my own eye.

Before everyone is done eating, Remy puts his fork down and stares at me. "Why are you doing this, man?"

I stand and face him down. "You wanna go over it right here in front of everyone?"

He looks down. "No."

"I didn't think so." Everyone is staring at us, and Lola is trying to keep a brave face, but she's struggling. "Eat!"

My family snaps out of their staring and returns to chatter while we eat.

Remy stands and walks away early. Sutton watches him walk away then returns to sending me dirty looks.

My parents look concerned but disregard it to talk to Henry. "Did you like the yams, Henry?" my mom asks him.

"I love them."

Sutton smacks her napkin on the table, stands, and walks toward the living room where Remy is watching TV.

Lola hasn't said a word through dinner, but her eyes have slowly darkened and her mouth has grown drawn.

After we help clear the dishes, I grab Loralei's hand and march right to Remy and Sutton. "Let's work it out in the octagon."

Remy ignores me and stares at the TV. I smack him upside the back of his head. "I said let's go work it out."

He glances up at me over his shoulder then sends a dismissive look to Loralei again. "Not worth it."

I smack him a lot harder, and his head bobs forward. "Ow."

He lurches up and back to take a swipe at me but misses when I duck. I throw my arm out to hit his temple, but he blocks it.

"You ready to fight?" I ask him.

"Yeah." He puts down the remote and stands up from the couch. He gives me an evil glare as he walks past Lola.

"This really isn't necessary," Lola says, but it's way too late for that. He's disrespected both of us, and he needs to pay for it.

I follow him out and hear my mom say, "What's going on?"

My parents and everyone else follows us out.

I hop up onto the platform of the homemade octagon we have in the outdoor gym. I whip off my shirt and Remy copies after he enters the cage with me. We're both wearing jeans, which are not great for kicking, but comfortable enough for fighting. Lola grabs the cage with her fingertips. "Don't worry. It's—"

A thump hits the back of my head. Remy took a cheap shot paying me back for what I did inside. I turn around and glare at him. "Now we're even."

"Oh then we're done here?" He holds up both hands, palms up. It's his last ditch effort to get out of this. Signaling his hands are empty. We don't have to fight.

My hands curl up into fists. "Not yet. You're gonna apologize to Loralei by the end of this."

"Pfft. She's the one who owes a huge apology to all of us."

I step up to him and get in his face. "Did you ever stop and think why she did what she did?"

"You brought in her dad? So we all pay for years?"

"Yeah. Then her dad died in prison. It screwed her up. She blamed me."

"And now she doesn't?" He circles me, showing me he's getting ready to fight.

"She forgave me. We're good. She's with me now."

"With you?" He stands and glares at me.

"She's mine. She's gonna be here. Accept it, or we'll fight like this every Sunday until you do."

"You'd fight me over her?"

"We're in here, aren't we?" Another reason we need this fight. I need to make it clear I'm serious. To him and everyone else including Loralei. There's a lot at stake here. I don't know when she became so important to me, but she has, and I'm saying it out loud right now for the first time.

"If you're going to do this, at least put on some gear." My mom steps up next to Lola. She looks less worried and more frustrated that another dinner is going to end in an unscheduled fight. She wants us to wear helmets, chest pads, and gloves, but she should know there's no stopping the Volcano when he's fired up. This is my moment with Remy, and we fight underground style, like my dad did back in New York. My dad walks up and makes eye contact with both of us before giving a slight nod that he's okay with this.

"No pads. No rules," I say.

Remy grunts in agreement.

I hear a few more grumbles from the onlookers, but my attention is all focused on him. I've fought Remy a hundred times. His weakness is his eyes tell where he's going to hit. He's too calculating and reveals his plan. His gaze is on my chest now, so I know where he's going. Sure enough, he breaks out with a heel kick to my chest. I grab his ankle and wrench his leg till he falls to the floor with a thump. He scrambles up and glares at me, shocked I'd take him down in the first ten seconds of fighting him.

"You look scared, Rem. What're you afraid of?" I stalk toward him, puffing my shoulders up, arm out wide to the sides

MEMORIZING MACE 131

and back. That would make any normal man shit his pants, but Remy's known me since we were scrawny teens, so I can't intimidate him with my size.

I throw a punch with my right and scrape his cheek as he's bobbing down. I try to get him with my left, but he's charging and knocking me back with his shoulder in my gut. We hit the mat and start swinging. I nail him several times in the ribs. He has the advantage being on top, and he throws a round of rapid punches to my face.

I can vaguely hear Sutton protesting, but it doesn't matter what anyone says. I'll take whatever Remy dishes out right now.

He leans back and nails my cheek so hard I'm seeing white. Shit. I can't move, but he keeps pummeling me. I hear Lola screaming "Stop!"

Remy lets up and stands. We're both panting and reeling from the shots we got in. He's winning so far.

I stand, but I'm unsteady on my feet. The rage inside me boild over, and suddenly I have the strength of a thousand men. I charge and nail him to the wire cage. I shoot punch after punch to his face. He blocks his face with his hands so I attack his ribs. I won't kill him, but I'm gonna leave some bruises, so we never have to do this again.

"Stop!" Sutton has jumped into the octagon. She's pulling on my arm. "He didn't know."

"Back off, Sutton." I push her away, so I can get back to pummeling Remy.

"But he didn't know who she was when he slept with her."

Hold up. Remy stills. I can't move. *He didn't know who she was when he slept with her?*

Someone gasps and whimpers at the side of the octagon. It's Loralei. She has her hand over her mouth, her eyes terrified.

I turn to look at Sutton. She's standing with her arms reaching out toward Remy like she wants to grab him away from me.

"He slept with her?" I'm stunned.

Sutton just stares back at me.

"Jesus, Sutton." Remy straightens and runs a hand through his hair.

"You didn't know?" Sutton asks me.

"Fuck no." I turn my gaze to Remy. "You slept with her?"

"A long time ago. It was nothing." He's trying to blow it off, but this is huge.

"Bullshit, Remy. You should've told me. Is that why you're so against her being here?"

Remy shakes his head, but I know it's true. He didn't want me to find out what happened.

"I was drunk. I wanted to make someone jealous. She was there so..." He shrugs like his dick just fell into Lola's pussy on accident.

"Fuck!" I turn away from the whole scene. Red hot magma pulses through my body. Under pressure and ready to blow. If she slept with my brother, that means he's seen her naked. He's touched her skin. He's been someplace I thought was my own. For once, I had someone to call mine, and he slept with her. He didn't know who she was, but...

I turn around and glare at Lola. "You knew who he was."

Her face is bright red, her shoulders stiff. She looks left and right, then turns away. She's humiliated. That means it's true. It's fucking true!

"Mace, stay calm." My mom's voice sounds so distant. She's trying to rein in the inferno, but it's pointless. Once the volcano erupts, you can't push the lava back in. The destruction is inevitable.

Lola strides toward her car. There's no way in hell she's leaving here alone.

I jump out of the cage and chase after her. "Lola!"

She rushes faster, breaking into a jog as she's reaching into her pocket for her keys.

"Lola!" My voice is a deep, angry roar. She's not fucking leaving.

She ignores me and makes it to her car door. She's trying to open it when I reach her and grab her keys. "You're not leaving."

She doesn't look at me. "I am! Give me my keys."

"You slept with my brother?"

She flinches back, shaking her head.

"You knew who he was. You fucked him and didn't tell me? I can't understand that. Explain it to me. How does that happen?"

She lowers her head. "Please. Let me leave."

"All of this was bullshit? Some new ploy to get revenge?"

"No." She finally looks up at me, and her eyes are glossy with tears about to spill.

"You planned all this? Are you trying to destroy me? Tie me down?" I'm spitting fire now, and I can't stop. It's hurting her. I don't care. "I trusted you. All this crap about forgiveness. Holy fucking shit. I had you all wrong. You really are wicked."

She swallows, and her eyes harden. "Give me my keys." She glares up at me, no longer hurt. She's angry now. Good. I'm angry too.

"When did this happen?"

"After my father died." Her eyes squint and shoot daggers at me. She's blaming me for his death again.

Suddenly I'm aware of my surroundings. We're having this fight in front of everyone. "Come back to my cabin. We're not doing this out here."

"I'm leaving, Mace. You forced me to come here. I told you no. This is not what I wanted." She throws her hands up and looks at the night sky like she's so frustrated she can't even look at me. "You're out of control. Nothing you do makes sense. No plan. No logic. You just walk around crudely reacting, not caring who gets hurt by it."

You're out of control. That's what people always say before they try to change me. I can't help who I am, and I can't be with anyone who doesn't accept me. "You know what? This isn't what I wanted either. You run back to your boring, safe life. Follow all the rules. Look where it's gotten you."

She growls and grits her teeth. "So we're back where we started? I hate you and you hate me? Fine!" She reaches out, grabs my wrists, and knees me in the balls. I buckle over from the red hot pain, and she snags her keys.

She jumps in her car, and the engine revs like an ugly exclamation mark at the end of her kick to my nards. "Leave me alone, Mace. I don't need you. I don't need anybody."

She glares up at me one last time before she closes the door.

Somehow, once again, I'm the twenty-year old asshole who took her virginity and locked up her dad. She's the psycho vindictive bitch. How easily we fall back into our old roles.

She backs out rough and spits up gravel in her hurry to escape.

What the fuck just happened? I turn stiffly and face my family. Most of them have left. Only Remy and Sutton stayed to watch my life fall apart. My parents are behind them.

I don't even want to kill Remy anymore. I'm mad at Loralei, and I'm furious with myself for screwing this up.

"Not a word," I mutter as I march past them, my balls aching where she nailed me, my heart bleeding where she tore a gash in it.

Chapter 13 Help Me, Dad

Loralei

I haven't cried so hard since my dad died. How could Mace have come to mean so much to me in such a short time? I know the answer. It wasn't a short time. It's been a long time. Since I first met him, I loved him.

It's so hard to admit to myself. I did honestly hate him, but I also loved him. We always straddled that line, even if it was only in my head. When reality offered to jump over to the love side, I gave him my body again. It was fantastic like the first time, like I'd dreamed it would be, and he shredded my heart again like I knew he would.

Returning to my house, I'm broken. I've lost my job, my dad, my self-respect, and now I have a man named after Satan out to get me. What do I have left? I have no pets, no friends, no one I can turn to.

That's my choice. I've isolated myself since my dad died. I buried myself in my work. Pinned my hopes on a loser like Griffin. I pull my car into my driveway and rest my head on the wheel. "Help me, Dad."

He doesn't respond, so I drag my butt up the stairs to my place.

Something feels off right away. My security light doesn't click on. A weird darkness surrounds the house, and something blocks the window.

Shoot. I don't have a gun. If someone is in there, I'm fighting with my fists.

I carefully open the door. Inside, even without the light on, I can see it's trashed. Coffee table turned up, couch on its side, stuff scattered all over the floor. When I turn on the light, shocking red paint marks everything. The couch has been slashed and painted red. I check the dining room. No one here. The hallway pictures are all smashed. I'm afraid to look in my bedroom. My precious sanctuary.

Oh God. It's even worse in my bedroom. They've taken my pictures from under my bed and sprayed them red.

My life board is trashed.

Someone has come in and erased my life.

I drop to my knees and cry. This was all I had. It wasn't much. It was humble and simple, but it was mine. Everything in this place I bought with my own money. Now it's all gone.

I'm not sure if it's an angel or just the old records in my head, but I hear my dad's voice now. "*Turn this challenge on its head. Take it and make it your victory because pain is brought to us to make us stronger, so fight through it and find your purpose on the other side of the battle field.*"

I don't know how to do that. I don't know how to turn this around.

I cry on the floor until the sobbing ebbs and my dad's words finally penetrate. He's right. I could be on the precipice of something big. I'm supposed to learn something from this. "Okay, Dad. No more hiding."

Even though my heart is broken, I'm not going to pine away for Mace anymore. That got me nowhere. I'm going to go out. Live life. Take chances. I have indefinite time off work. I've never travelled alone. I'm going to drain my savings and hit the road. My journey is waiting for me. I can't sit in my apartment anymore obsessing over my job. I'm going for it.

The second I stand, fear grips me again. What if I get in trouble? Will I ruin the family name? Isn't it already ruined by my dad? What if Diablo finds me when I'm alone, and I won't have Mace to protect me? What if I do something so stupid, and I don't get my job back? It doesn't matter. It can't be worse than what's already happening. I've lost my job. I don't have Mace to protect me. Might as well go for it for once in my life. I don't even know what going for it means, but I know I have to try.

Before I can talk myself out of it, I pack anything I can into a few bags and take off in my car. Tonight I'll stay in a hotel. Tomorrow, who knows? I'm not going to plan it out. I'll take it day by day.

Chapter 14 Check-In

Mace

I am out of whiskey. Again. How hard is it to stock up on Jack Daniels? I'll never learn. I make the same damn mistake over and over.

Someone knocks at my cabin door. "Mace?"

Cutter.

"You bring me a fifth of Jack?"

"No. Check-in. Open up."

Fucking check-in. Another word for big brother nosing into my business. Passing down his judgment and advice from a guy who's just as messed up in the head as I am.

"I'm here too, Mace. Let us in."

I groan at the sound of Sutton's voice. I love Cutter and his biological sister, who is now my sister too, but sometimes they need to learn when to stay away. Let me drink and wallow alone in my cabin.

"Go away!"

I know I'm being a dick, but I'm dead inside. I have nothing to say to Cutter and Sutton right now.

Cutter opens the door and walks in. Well, shit. Guess I forgot to lock it.

He glares down at me. "No more skipping your check-in."

How many have I skipped? I've lost track of time. Does it even matter anymore?

"What's she doing here?" I give Sutton the side eye because younger siblings don't normally attend check-ins with older ones.

"I'm worried about you, Mace." Her voice is soft and gentle, but also condescending as hell.

"I'm fine." I fall back onto the couch and stare at the ceiling. "Except I'm outta booze. Go get me a bottle of Jack."

"Get your ass up and talk to me." Cutter pokes at the nearly dead fire in my fireplace. He throws a log on and moves it around till it catches.

"I got nothing to say."

"Bullshit. You've been moping around here since before Thanksgiving. What's going on?"

"What the fuck do you think is going on?"

He's still crouching in front of the fire, looking at me like I'm a petri dish growing fungus. "This about Loralei?"

Sutton crosses her arms, and her head bobs back and forth as I talk to Cutter.

I sit up and rub my face, trying to shake some of this stupor off me. "Isn't everything about Loralei?"

"I'm sorry about... ya know. Bringing up Remy," Sutton says.

We haven't talked about it since that night, and I'm not interested in doing it now.

"Do not mention it again. Hear me? I don't care what she did in her past. It's a non-issue for me. If you and Remy got a problem with it, go work it out, but don't ever bring it to me."

Sutton nods. "Okay. I just... I feel bad."

"Yeah? Not worse than me." I blew it big time with her. Now it's too late.

Cutter stands up and towers over me like he's superior now that he has Cass. He got lucky with her, but it doesn't make him the patron saint of the Twists. "Call the girl so we can all stop worrying about you." He swipes some food wrappers off the floor and tosses them into the trash.

"Believe me, I've thought about it non-stop. I'm not calling her."

"Why not? You're obviously hooked on her. Making yourself miserable. Get her ass up here."

I shake my head. "I'm a tumbleweed made of razor blades. I'll blow through her life and chop it up again."

"You don't think you can make it with her?" He sits down on the couch next to me and leans back.

"I don't think it's fair to her. I'm not gonna settle down. I'll always be out of control. She's not gonna roll with me."

"Did you give her a chance?"

"No."

He huffs and shakes his head. "She might be up for a roll with a tumbleweed made of razor blades. Some girls like danger. Never woulda thought a good girl like Cass would go for a scarred monster with an obsession for knives. Turns out she's perfect for me. We made it work."

"That's all nice for you, Cut. I'm not you, and she's not Cass."

He pats my shoulder. "Mace, we love you either way. You go with this girl, we'll accept her. You move on and keep rolling the way you always have, we still love you. Unconditional. That's what we are."

I look down and let that sink in. The best part is I know he means it. "That helps, bro."

Sutton leans down and wraps her arms around me. She doesn't usually hug me, so this one cracks my shell. "I love you,

Mace. You're my brother too. I want to see you happy. If she makes you happy, I want her to be with you."

When she pulls away, I look up at her. "She doesn't make me happy. She makes me grounded."

They both freeze and stare at me. Sutton gasps. "She makes you grounded?"

"Yep. Only woman in the world who stops the chaos in my head. Never thought I'd see the day. She had me showing up on time. I planned ahead. She was a good influence on me." Now I'm lost without her.

"Oh, you need to go get her." Sutton laughs.

"There's no miracle cure for who I am. You pin a tumbleweed in place, it still won't grow."

"You got some messed up thoughts in there, Mace." Cutter stands and checks the fire before walking to the door. "But I feel ya. You know I get that."

Cutter's words are hitting home. "I appreciate that you care, but please just leave me alone to sort this out."

"I'm not giving up on you." Cutter gives me his serious face. "I know you're capable of it. Remember those first few years with Mom and Dad, we all fought it. They didn't give up. You came around and let them love you. I think that was about the time you were with Loralei."

Oh man, Cutter's going for the jugular. Cass has him talking about his feelings and shit. He's right, of course. The first time I ever accepted someone's love was when I was twenty, shortly after I had my encounter with Loralei. "You got me thinking."

"Yeah, man. Don't let the messed up thoughts take over. Be open to possibilities."

I nod and he lifts his chin. Sutton gives me one last worried look before they leave.

I love them, and they know me. It's true I never asked Loralei if she would be happy by my side. Her inner lioness probably would, but will Lola let her loose? Only one way to find out.

Cutter walks back in alone. "Got news."

"What?"

"The FBI found three bodies on the island. Loralei reported Diablo as her kidnapper. They're still looking for Giselle, but they think Arthur might have been using that island to move drugs. The girls were the mules."

"And Diablo was the supplier."

"Possibly."

"Was one of the girls named Hannah Clark?" I ask him.

"Yeah."

"That's the girl Loralei was looking for."

"She can stop looking now." He nods and closes the door again.

"Shit."

***

The bloodied and bruised skip coughs as I drop him in a chair in Wayne's office. "Here he is. Failure to show. Pay up."

Wayne's handlebar moustache wiggles as he scans the guy. "He looks beat up."

"He fell."

"The last skip was beat up too, Volcano."

"I've been clumsy."

"Right." He stands and walks toward the skip. "C'mon, buddy. I got a place you can wait while I get the truck ready to take you in."

The guy grunts as Wayne walks him back to a room he uses as a holding cell.

It's been fifty days without seeing or hearing from Loralei. Every second of the holidays sucked without her there. I missed her yams at Christmas, missed kissing her on New Year's. Why? Why did I let her go? Beating the crap out of fugitives isn't helping. Nothing will help but seeing her again.

Wayne returns and gives me a disapproving look. "What's going on?"

"Guy's an asshole. Owes tons of child support. Doesn't show up for his hearings."

"I'm asking about you."

I sit down in the chair opposite his desk. "You remember Loralei Valentine from back in the day? Emrick's daughter?"

"The crazy bitch who kept coming back for revenge?" He's shuffling through the papers on his desk, reacting without thinking. Still, it pulls on my nerves hearing him talk about her like that.

"Since we go way back, I'm gonna let that one slide, but I'm giving you notice. Things have changed. She's a good girl. We've forgiven each other, and I'd appreciate it if you don't bring up the past."

He stops shuffling and folds his arms on his desk as he levels his gaze on mine. "I'm surprised to hear you talk like this, Mace. Not like you to take up a cause for a woman."

"She'd been kidnapped, couldn't remember what happened. I helped her retrace her steps to get it back. By the time she did, I was falling for her." I haven't said it out loud to anyone, but now that I have, I know it's true.

He nods and raises his eyebrows. This is not the way I normally talk, and he has a smile brewing under his mustache waiting to taunt me.

"Anyway, haven't seen her in over a month."

"Who's fault is that?"

"Mine. All mine."

"You might wanna go see the girl so you can stop assaulting people for skipping bail."

"Went to see her. No one there. Her car's gone. Not returning my calls. Been searching for her. Worried Diablo got to her."

"Give me her picture and some contacts. I'll send out a BOLO for her."

"No. I don't want to draw attention to her like that. I'll find her myself." Wayne's eyes narrow in on my fingers, which are tapping on his desk. I didn't even know I was doing it. I run my hands through my hair, trying to cover.

"It's okay, Mace. I know you fidget. I don't mind."

"I shouldn't do it."

"Who says? It's who you are. Your fingers tap, your knee bounces. All that energy is what makes you a damn good bounty hunter. Quick and alert. Don't be ashamed of it." He's back to looking through papers on his desk. "I was gonna send you out after this guy next, but I already gave it to Helix, and you're busy looking for Loralei." He sets a folder aside.

"Helix doing more bounties and less hits?"

"It looks like Helix may have fallen under the spell of a woman too. There must be some voodoo in the air. Oh, how the mighty have fallen."

"Helix? Impossible. The man has no heart."

"I might've said the same about you five minutes ago. Now that I think about it, I don't really know if he's involved with her. Maybe they're just working together. He gave Leona half his cut on the last skip."

"Leona?"

"Leona Hart. You heard of her?"

"I haven't, but the name sounds familiar." I could swear I heard that name or read it somewhere. "It could be Loralei."

"Why would you say that?"

"I call her lioness. Leona. Hart, Valentine. Helix knows her. They'd been communicating. It has to be her."

His brows draw together, and he leans forward. "Helix is baggin' your girl?"

My fingernails dig into his wood desk. "He'd better not be, or he'll face the Volcano."

"You boys don't kill each other. You both make me a lot of money."

"I'm not going to have to kill him because he's smart enough not to fuck with me, and Loralei would never sleep with him."

"I hope you're right." He tosses the folder my way. "Go get her."

I check out the file and the picture. "Bobby Morrison. Twenty-five grand for his return. Nice. This his mother's address?"

"Looks like it."

I tuck the folder under my arm. "Thank you, Wayne."

"I didn't do nothing."

"You did more than you know."

MEMORIZING MACE

I tap his desk twice more and head out of his office. Helix and Lola together. If they're fucking, I'm going to bash his face. I might even bash his face if they're not because screw him for not telling me he was in contact with Lola knowing I've been going insane looking for her. The man lied to my face. Said he hadn't seen her. Helix is about to find out what happens when you lie to the Volcano.

***

I'm parked outside Bobby's mother's house when it hits me. I didn't hear the name before, but I read it on the dark web. I passed over it quickly, but I did read something about Leona Hart.

Logging in on my burner phone, it takes me a while to find it. Here it is.

A bounty on Leona Hart. Five hundred grand alive, a million dead. Well shit.

After another hour staking out Bobby Morrison's mother's house, I'm not any calmer when he finally comes out. His hair's standing up, and he's wearing pajama bottoms and an old ratty T-shirt. He gets into a red Challenger, and I pull out behind him.

A truck with two people in it falls in line behind me. Fuck. Yep. Lola and Helix are trailing him too. This should be fun.

We end up at a house in downtown Sacramento. Bobby parks and enters through the front door, but I pull around to the alley and break in through a back door.

Bobby is walking down the hallway when I catch him and hold his arms behind his back. "You missed your bail hearing, Bobby."

"What? No. It's next week."

"It was last week, and you were a no-show. So I'm gonna bring you to Wayne, and you can explain it all to him."

"C'mon, man. I got a kid."

"Yeah, a kid you're doing a shitty job of role modeling for. All you gotta do is pay your child support, show up to your hearings, and act like a mature adult. You can't do that?"

"I can, it's just..."

There's a knock at the door. I need to lock up Bobby somewhere, so I can deal with Helix. There's a big hamper in the corner, like the kind you find at a hotel for dirty linens.

"I'm gonna need you to wait in here for a while."

"What? In the hamper?"

"It'll just be a minute."

"No."

I lift him between his legs, hoist him in, and shut it. He screams and bangs on the lid.

"Be quiet."

"But—"

I open the lid and punch him hard in the face. He shuts up. "Good boy."

Helix bangs on the door. "Bobby! Need to talk to you."

I hide behind the door before Helix kicks it open. When he walks in, I nail him with a surprise punch to the jaw.

He flashes into fight mode instantly, not even looking to see who hit him.

I block and punch, but he's strong like a robot. My fists bounce off his metal head, and he's not showing any signs of feeling pain.

I sweep his legs and he falls on his stomach. I hop on his back and pin his hands to the floor.

"What the fuck, Mace?"

"You sell her out?"

"What?" He grunts and tries to get up.

"You told Diablo about Leona Hart."

"I did not."

"You told me you hadn't seen her."

"She asked me to do that. Get off me, asshole." He gouges my thigh with his elbow and bucks his hips, throwing me forward over his head.

I'm struggling to get him back under control when Loralei enters the room from the hallway. She's holding a taser gun and pointing it at us. She looks hot as hell in black leather pants, jacket, heeled boots, fierce hair and makeup.

"You gonna tase me, Lola?" This is it. The test. If she tases me, she's screwing Helix and we're done. I'll never be able to trust her.

If she doesn't tase me, she's badass, hot as hell, not screwing him, and I want her by my side.

Everything hinges on what she does next.

Chapter 15 Jealousy

Loralei

My ears buzz and my heart flatlines.

Mace has Helix pinned.

His hair hides his face, but his arms are taut with the pressure of holding Helix down.

"You gonna tase me, Lola?" I can barely hear Mace repeat his question.

"What're you doing here?" My voice wobbles.

"I'm taking Bobby in." He's wearing his fringe jacket and torn black jeans. He looks so damn sexy. My body feels instantly pulled toward him like I want to jump his bones, not tase him.

"No, you're not. Twenty-five grand says I'm taking him in." Oh no. Mace is not going to steal this bounty from me.

"You're a bounty hunter now?" He chuckles.

"Yes, and this is my skip, so get out of here, and let me do my job."

Helix squirms under Mace. "Let me up, asshole."

"You want Bobby, then tase me, and I'll let Helix up, you get your man." Mace's dark intense eyes taunt me. He's daring me to betray him. I should do it. He's hurt me many times, and this is my chance to get even. But no. I can't.

I see Mace in my mind all the time, but seeing him in real life is like standing at the base of a skyscraper. He's so massive, he eclipses everything in the room. I should hate him, yet I feel weak in the knees and excited to see him.

I lower my taser. "I'm not gonna do that."

"Good." He struggles with Helix until they both stand.

"What the hell is going on?" Helix pushes Mace, but he doesn't budge.

Mace pulls his shoulders back, and he's spitting fumes. "You tell me. Are you fucking Loralei?"

"I wish I was, but the girl is hooked on some other dude."

Mace squints and glances from Helix to me. "Then what're you doing with her?"

"He's training me, Mace. I can be working with him and not screwing him."

He just glares back at me like he doesn't believe me. God, I hate him.

"Where's Bobby?" Helix looks around the room.

"He's in the hamper." Mace points at a box without looking at it. He keeps his eyes on me.

"What's he doing in there?" Helix walks over to the box.

"He's being quiet."

Helix chuckles, but Mace and I are locked in a staring match.

"You can have Bobby if you take him and leave now," Mace says to Helix.

Helix puts his hands on his hips. "You okay with that Loralei?"

Part of me wants to say no and fight with Mace over Bobby, but a bigger part wants to be alone with him. "Yep. See you later, Helix."

Helix walks over to the laundry bin, opens it, and looks inside. "Let's go." He lifts Bobby out and plants him on his feet. Bobby stumbles as Helix leads him out the front door. "Bye,

Loralei. You wanna catch more bad guys, you call me." He signs off with a wave.

"I will."

Mace growls as Helix leaves and closes the door behind him.

Just like that, I'm alone with Mace.

"You didn't tase me," he says with wonder in his voice.

"No."

"Why not? You and Helix would get Bobby and the money, leave me reeling on the floor."

"I wouldn't do that to you. That's not who I am, and I'm offended you'd think I would."

"You didn't sleep with Helix?" I can hear the jealousy scrape in his throat like he has a claim to me, but he doesn't.

"If I did, would it bother you? Drive you wild with jealousy?"

His jaw tightens, and a vein in his neck throbs. "Who's this other guy you're hooked on?" He takes a cautious step toward me like he's hunting a skittish doe.

I cross my arms and pop a knee. His eyes lock on my hips and flare with heat. He's as affected by me as I am by him, but I have the advantage. I'm going to play with him. "No one you know." I raise my chin and challenge him.

"Hmm." His lips curl. "It's not someone you used to hate?"

Great. Now he's playing with me. "No." I try to keep my voice strong, but he has me figured out, and with his cobalt eyes locked on mine, it's quite a challenge.

"Did this mystery someone help you regain your memory? Maybe rescue you from an island?"

"It's not you, Mace. Totally vain of you to suggest it." I press my lips together to hide my smile, but the glint in his eyes tells me he knows I'm lying.

"Maybe it's the guy who fucked you on top of a mountain and made you scream his name into the Great Basin?" He's close enough now he could reach out and grab me. "The only man that brings out the lioness in you." He's full-on grinning now.

"The lioness is out full-time lately."

"Oh, really? I like that." He wraps a hand around my waist and tugs, but I stand strong. If I fall into his arms, I'm done. I won't be able to resist him. He steps so close our breath mingles, and the heat from his body caresses my skin. I step back, but he pulls me up against his chest. "I've been looking for you."

"Oh really?"

"Was worried about you."

"Here I am. Safe and sound."

"I see that. You look fucking fantastic."

"I know." It's like my body was made to wear leather pants. I'd never tried them before, but now that I have, I'll never go back to jeans or slacks.

"What the hell happened to you? Where's the headbands and anchor scarfs?" His gaze travels over my cleavage, which is visible in this tight black shirt with criss-cross straps over the front.

"Nothing happened to me. I'm out of work indefinitely. I needed some money. I have the skills. I called up Helix and he's mentoring me." I shrug like this is simple when I know it's totally not.

"Helix is a hitman."

"Well, he agreed not to kill anyone when I was training with him."

He tilts his head. "He only agreed because he thought you were gonna fuck him."

"How do you know that?"

"Trust me. He may look like a machine, but he's a man under there. No man could look at you and not want to fuck you." He smirks, and I hate it that he looks so darn good doing it too.

"Either way. This is who I am now, and you can back off, so I can get out of here and back to work." I push on his shoulders, but he's solid as a redwood.

"I'm not done talkin' yet." He pushes me, and we shuffle backward until my butt hits an old wooden armoire with a desk and a big oval mirror. "I was looking for you for a reason." He leans down to line his lips up with mine. He's just a breath away from kissing me.

"And I suppose now you're going to tell me what that is whether I want to hear it or not."

"That's right." He mashes his hips into mine, and my butt digs into the wood. "You may not want to hear it, but I'm gonna say it. I shoulda said it when I had a chance, but I blew it."

"I'm listening."

He looks down like he's struggling to find the words. I hold my breath and watch him. When he looks up, his eyes have turned a darker blue, almost black, and his mouth is a firm line. "I don't give a shit what happened with Remy."

My gasp fills the air between us. "You don't?"

He shakes his head slightly. "I don't care what happened in the past. It's forgotten. Right now, I want you with me. My family is gonna learn to accept you for me because they'll see you're the one who makes me happy."

"I do?"

His hand, still in my hair, cups the back of my head and brings my face closer to his. "There's something happening between us, and I won't let anything get in the way." He strokes my hair and squeezes my neck. "I like everything about you. Anchors, scarfs, wicked evil, sweet cop, tempting lioness. It was never what happened with Remy. It was me being stupid not wanting to accept I'd fallen for you."

"Wow."

My spine tingles as he works his fingers up into my hair. "I'm not a settling down man. I need to roam."

I huff a laugh. "I see no lies here."

He presses a brief kiss to my lips as he smiles. "I think you want to roam with me."

"I might like that," I concede.

"I want to work through whatever bullshit we have to because I think if I could find a woman to give my heart to, it'd be you."

Okay. These words coming from Mace, who always seemed so closed and distant, are rocking me to my core. I didn't know he had it in him. "I can't believe you're saying this." My voice is a whisper.

"Neither can I." His smile grows wider. "I missed you bad. Not just the physical. I missed all of you."

My lips sputter, and I have to hold back a sob. "I missed you too."

"So come back up to Pleasure Mountain with me."

Mace makes it sound so easy, but... "Your family..."

"They'll support it. They know you're who I want."

"Wow."

"I'm gonna kiss you now, Leona." He presses his closed mouth to mine. The tightness of his lips, the passion in his eyes is so honest and hungry. The kind of kiss that curls your toes and weakens your knees at the thought of what it means. He said he cares for me, and the kiss reinforces his words like the echo of a promise, the chorus of a song repeating, but building and crescendoing.

I'm not gonna fight him on this. I want to be back with him. I want to roam with him.

His lips part and suck me in greedily like he was eyeing a box of cookies and finally gave into the temptation to devour them.

He lifts me by my thighs and something falls to the floor as he plops me on top of the armoire. He moves in, and I tilt my head and arch my back to keep contact with his mouth. I work his massive arms out of his jacket and swipe his shirt up. He helps me get it over his head, and I'm faced with the hairy chest of the man of my dreams. He smells like a delicious manly conglomeration of sweat, soap, and possibly the acidic linger of beer.

My fingertips explore the grooves and sinewy muscles of his back. Every inch of him is covered in taut, solid iron like he's made of metal and not skin and bones.

With a deep hoarse groan, he breaks the kiss and trails his lips down my cheek, my neck, my chest. For a man with a body of iron, his lips are silky soft, just a hint of saliva wetting my skin and leaving a tingle behind, not sloppy, uncontrolled licking like some men.

His hands tug and stretch the fabric of my shirt until my breasts are exposed. He pulls one nipple into his mouth through the lace of my bra, and his tortured moan reverberates in my soul like a drum.

"God, Mace." I wrap my hands around his head and pull him closer as he teases my nipple with his lips and tongue. I want him so badly, my skin sizzles and shakes with thirst for him.

His massive, rock-hard cock presses urgently between my thighs, demanding entry that is blocked by the clothes we're still wearing.

His hand grabs my butt cheek and squeezes. "These pants. Off." He maintains the kiss as he fusses with the buttons.

In his impatience with my leather pants, we topple to the hardwood floor, his arms cushioning my fall as he lands on top of me. He's a man on a mission and attacks the closure to my pants again. I can barely pay attention to the details, but somehow he gets them open and I raise my hips, allowing him to yank them down my legs. They get stuck on my boots, and he leaves them there. He rips my underwear and dives in with his mouth. The hair on his chin tickles my thighs as his curly hair creates a privacy screen like we're under a blanket instead of in the middle of some random living room.

My fingers twine in his hair as he slowly presses his tongue flat and gentle against my clit, then rolls and flicks. He repeats this motion harder and faster, bringing me higher to the verge of crying. My hips rise up and I realize my legs are strapped together by my pants, preventing me from wrapping them around him. The physical limitation is maddening. I'm aching for him to go deeper, wanting to be consumed by him until neither one of us remains separate, only one body writhing and pulsing as one.

At the worst possible time, without warning, he pulls away and presses his wet lips to my navel, circling his tongue there in a vicious imitation of what he was doing.

My voice comes out pleading and strangled. "Mace!"

"Not yet, babe." Thankfully, he's unzipping my boots and working my pants all the way off.

Once my legs are free, I kick his hips and force him onto his back. He laughs as I climb on top of him and grab the top button of his jeans.

"Two can play at that game." I have his pants open and good Lord, he was commando under there. It's like opening a present that keeps on giving. He's all man and fully turned on.

I drop down and pull the tip of his giant cock between my lips, open, and slip down. I use my hand to crank the bottom of his shaft because it's so big there's no way it will all fit in my mouth.

He throws his head back and moans. "Fuck, Lola. You suck my cock so goddamn good. Don't stop."

That reminds me of the trick he pulled on me, so to pay him back, I stop. I sit up and smile at him as I wipe my lower lip. I'm breathing heavy and my lips part.

His eyes widen and he looks down confused, then his lips spread into a wicked grin. He does a sit up, grabs me by my ass, and we're up and flying around the room again.

We land back on the armoire with the mirror. He pierces me with his giant cock and I'm transported. This is too good. I'm in a place where he can keep pumping into me for hours, and I'll never want him to stop.

I bounce up and down on his dick, and he pulls his lips back over his teeth. His frame tightens like he's fighting off a freight train.

A monumental force pushes through me, stealing my breath and sending me out of my body and straight to heaven. Only Mace. Never has anyone else made me come like this.

Before I can recover, he pulls out, turns me around to face the mirror, and lifts me up by my waist. His strong arms slam me down on his shaft. "God, look at you."

I'm sitting with my knees spread on an armoire, still reeling from an orgasm, looking at my naked body getting fucked from behind by Mace and his giant dick. My breasts are red and heaving, and he's biting my shoulder as he watches in the mirror.

"Watch me ram into you."

My eyes fall closed as my head lolls back.

"Watch."

I force my attention back to the mirror. One of his hands moves down to my clit and massages it. The hair from his chest and his rock hard muscles rub against my back, and I'm suspended in Mace. He pinches my nipple. "Come hard for me, Lola. Give it to me." He adds a finger where his dick is thrusting in. His hand is so big, his palm is mashing my clit while his fingers thrust inside, and I'm captive in his arms. I'm helpless to stop him. I'm a writhing, living creature and nothing else matters.

I'm pulsing around him, and he's groaning in my ear. "I could watch you come like that forever. Don't stop."

And I'm not. It keeps coming and rolling through me in waves and grunts, forcing me to gasp for air. Somehow, I'm spinning again, and he's entering me from the front. His mouth smashes down on mine while his hips ram up into me. I am full of Mace. It feels like it'll never end as another orgasm builds deep in my core. "Oh my God." I can't believe this is happening.

"Yes. Yes, babe. I make you come again and again." His voice scratches. "You feel so good. So damn good," he murmurs against my lips. He growls and slams hard into the armoire until the glass is shaking. He's not watching anymore. His eyes are closed, but I can only imagine what we look like in the mirror. "You come alive for me. You fall apart for me. Got it? Only me."

"Yes, Mace."

He pulls my hair and my chin juts up. He's sucking and kissing all over it when he rams up and his hips spasm. He grunts and holds his breath, as we fall over the edge together.

With a final groan, his head collapses on my shoulder. He turns sideways, and his hot breath caresses my neck. "Mmm."

I'm purring, totally satisfied and stunned by the incredible presence of this man. I've dreamed of being with him like this for so long and now it's here, I can barely wrap my head around it.

"That was wicked evil, Mace. Why'd you do that?"

He chuckles. "Did you see the way your lioness came out to fight? That's why I did it. You light up like searchlights shining powerful beams into the night sky. I could watch it over and over."

I laugh too because he's right. It drove me wild and made it all the more earth shattering.

We stand there wrapped in each other for a long while. The sweat between us cools, and the sticky parts start to dry. He pulls away to kiss my lips. The virulent volcano is finally at rest.

MEMORIZING MACE 161

"I want more." He kisses my neck.

"Me too, but not here. We don't even know whose house this is."

We separate and fix our clothes. He picks his jacket up off the floor and grabs my hand. "Let's go home."

I squeeze his hand back and smile.

I'm a little nervous about going back to Twist Cabins, but somehow with Mace by my side, I feel invincible. We'll face whatever comes our way together.

Chapter 16 The Lone Ranger

When we get to his truck, Mace chuckles when he sees Helix has thrown my bag in the back. I guess Helix saw the writing on the wall.

On the way home, he reaches across the seat and tugs my shoulder closer until I'm cuddled up next to him. He's smiling with one hand casually draped over the wheel.

"You look happy." I'm stating the obvious, but it's different too. He's normally easy-going, but he has a joy in his eyes that wasn't there before. He's also noticeably not touching the radio stations.

"I am." He squeezes my shoulder and glances at me. "Do you know how hard it was to look for you while at the same time not drawing attention to you?"

"How long were you looking for me?"

"I knew right after you left I'd screwed it up. Started looking for you a week ago after a few words with my family."

"I'm still worried about going back. I don't want you to fight with them over me."

He looks at me and smiles. "They will accept you unconditionally this time. My mom forgave you the second she realized it was you on that helicopter. Most of the others came around when you showed up at dinner with yams. Remy and Sutton held onto that shit for their own twisted reasons. It had nothing to do with you and me. They need to work it out between themselves, and I told Sutton as much."

"That's awesome, Mace. Thank you. I'm really shocked you'd do all that for me."

"Nothing I wouldn't do for you. Stop being shocked and start accepting it. We're gonna see where this thing goes. If it keeps going the way it is, I can see us falling in love, making a life together. Shit. I'm shocked too, but my gut's guiding me on this one. We can't let it slip away over a stupid fight."

I snuggle into his chest and close my eyes. "All right."

"We do have a few issues to talk about."

Uh oh. "Okay."

"I want you to lay low at Twist Cabins for a while, until I take care of Diablo."

"What do you mean by that?"

"You know about the bounty on you?" He pats my shoulder to comfort me, but nothing can soften the blow of those words.

"There's a bounty on me?"

He shakes his head. "You didn't know? If you want to be a bounty hunter you gotta keep up on these things. Bounty on Leona Hart, million bucks dead, half a mil alive. I assume it's Diablo, and it's worth more to him to see you dead."

"Oh my God. Or it could be Giselle."

"True. So you can see why I wasn't pleased with you running around with Helix. He could turn on you and claim the money. He gets greedy, he'd kill you first and deliver the body."

An icy chill trickles down my spine. "I had no idea. I really think I can trust Helix. He never tried anything, and I was sleeping in his bed."

His arm grows stiff around me. "You slept in his bed?"

"He slept on the couch. Nothing happened. We can trust him."

"Verdict's out on Helix. I can't read him. He's like a damn robot. Also, Cutter's been in contact with the FBI on Arthur's case. The girl you were looking for, Hannah Clark, they found her body. She's dead."

My heart sinks and I gasp. "Where?"

"Little Santa Rosa Island. Three bodies buried out there. You would've been number four."

"What was going on on that island?"

"The FBI is chasing down Giselle. They have evidence Diablo shipped drugs through there and used women as mules. Some of them ended up dead, and he'd bury them there. That was the new job they had in store for you."

"I saw signs of that connection too, but I kept it to myself."

"You were snooping around asking about the missing girl. You make Diablo nervous anyway because of your dad."

"What do you mean about my dad?"

"Your dad bought drugs from him. It's possible your dad wasn't paying up and was threatening to flip on him when he got arrested and ended up dead."

Okay. This is too much. I sit up and pull away from him. "You think Diablo killed my dad?"

"It's possible. Or had someone do it. I wouldn't put it past him. He's sadistic and puts drugs and money over everything. You should see how messed up his kids are."

It's hard to process all the emotions at once. I'm sad, shocked, and angry. Mostly I'm angry. "I want him."

"Nope. Let the FBI or me and my brothers handle this. You're too close to it. You'll blow it."

My lips sputter, and I scoot even farther away from him. "Have you ever seen me blow it?"

"Which one of us refused to go the wrong way down a one-way street?" He gives me the side eye.

"That was a mental block. The memories." I cross my arms and stare out the window. He's making me angry, and we just got back together. I don't want to fight again.

"Sure."

He needs to understand what happened. "I would totally go the wrong way now. It was my memories stopping me. My mind didn't want to remember going the wrong way down a one-way street when he kidnapped me."

He growls. "I'm gonna kill that asshole."

"Now who's too close to it? You're not thinking rationally either."

"I never do. Doesn't stop me. It's different."

"It's not. Let me in on it, or I won't give you the intel I have."

"What do you have?"

"I have his entire phone. I conned his service provider to switch his data to another phone."

"You did?" His lip turns up and he looks impressed.

"I just needed his security information, and I found it all through research. The phone had passwords and emails I used to access his accounts. I put everything in a database. I can tell you anything you need to know about Marval Diablo Rios, but you have to include me in any plans."

"I don't make plans."

"The last time you went in without a plan, you ended up with a fistful of cocaine in your eyes. You could've lost your vision. Include me in this. I've been working this case. I have the intel and the training. The hit is on me. He killed my father, and now he wants me dead. You include me."

"No." His fingers start tapping on the wheel. We're both getting upset again, but this is important.

"Fine. I'll go after him myself."

"You will not."

"I'll do whatever I need to do. I'm a cop. Even worse, I'm a broke cop out of a job, there's a bounty on my head, and I have nothing to lose."

He pulls over to the side of the road, and the gravel crunches under the wheels as we roll to a stop. "Some things in your life are gonna change right now, and I'm gonna lay it out for you because you don't seem to be getting it. You're not the Lone Ranger anymore. At the hospital you said you didn't have anybody else. Now you do. You got me, and I come with a whole family. So you're not alone, and I don't want to hear you saying you got nothing to lose because I'm thinking if I lost you I'd lose everything."

"Okay." Mace keeps blowing me away. I want it to be true so badly. I move closer again and snuggle under his arm. "I don't want to lose you either."

"But you're right about being a cop and having the skills. We shouldn't exclude you. I know from watching my mom it's hard to keep a woman hell-bent on getting involved out of the way."

I nod.

"So we'll do this together. I'll let you plan it because you're right. Diablo is high up on the chain in the drug cartel, and he didn't get there by getting suckered."

"From what I can see from his phone, he's well-connected and doing high-dollar deals with a lot of famous people."

He nods and pulls the truck onto the mountain road up to Twist Cabins. After a few minutes he says, "You don't have to worry about money anymore. I'm funding this from here on out."

Mace keeps hitting me deep in the gut with his proclamations. "That's nice of you, but I support my half-siblings. I need to keep working doing the bounty hunting for them."

"You can't keep working with the bounty over your head. I'm lucky I got to you before they did. Your siblings will have whatever they need. I'll see to it."

"I can't ask that of you."

"It's already done. Accept it."

I want to fight him, but I know I'll lose. Mace is determined today, and all I can do is go along with it. If he wants to help me, I have to let him. "This is like a dream."

"This is only the beginning."

***

Back at Pleasure Mountain, he parks his truck and comes around to help me out of the passenger seat. "Can we sneak back to your cabin without being seen?"

"Probably not. Knowing my family they're watching us right now." He bends down to plant a kiss on my lips. "Let's give 'em something to talk about." He grabs my waist and dips me back as he deepens the kiss.

My body instantly lights up for him, and I don't care who's watching. I kiss him back with the fervor of a thousand giants. He wraps an arm behind my back, lifts me up and over his shoulder, and all I can see is his boots as he carries me up the hill caveman-style. Mace's entire family—if they're watching, which I'm not sure if they are because I can't see because I'm upside down—is now getting a first-person view of my butt in leather pants. This is not the way I wanted to come back to Twist Cabins.

Inside his cabin, he flips me over and plants me on my feet, but I'm up again in a second with my back against the door and Mace's huge body caging me in.

He's kissing me and ramming up into my core as I lock my feet together behind his back.

A knock sounds from outside. "Mace? It's Sutton."

"Go away."

"Dad wants me to ask if you can teach the haka tomorrow morning." I'd forgotten Mace sometimes teaches classes at his family's self-defense studio.

"You coulda texted me."

"Is Loralei here?"

"No," he barks back through the door.

"Please, I saw her with you. I really need to talk to her."

He growls and looks to the ceiling as he lowers me to the floor. He's floppy like a stubborn teen as he opens the door. He steps back until I'm face-to-face with Sutton.

"Loralei. I'm sorry. It wasn't fair what I did. I let my emotions take over, and I wasn't thinking rationally. The past is history. I need to let it go. Can we start again? I'd like us to be friends."

Okay. This family is too much. Do they talk about everything? So, I guess if I'm going to be part of this, I need to reciprocate. "I'm sorry too, about everything. I'd really like us to be friends too."

She hugs me. "Awesome." She smiles and looks from me to Mace, who is towering behind me with one hand on the door.

"We done here?"

"Oh, yeah, sure. See you tomorrow!" Sutton spins on her heels and walks away. Mace closes the door and scoops me up by my butt again. He carries me to the bedroom then into the bathroom. "Mace, you don't need to carry me. I can walk."

"But this is more fun."

After an hour of steamy shower sex, we're lying in bed wearing only towels. Mace rolls on top of me and kisses me.

"Your lips are swollen and red."

"Someone's been aggressively kissing me for hours now."

"Hmm. I wonder who."

"Could it be the man who rescued me off an island? Saved my life? Forgave me and helped me remember what I'd forgotten?"

"Sounds like a fantastic guy. A real keeper. Don't let him go."

I kiss him as I'm laughing. "I should get up and work on a plan to deal with Diablo." I push up on his shoulders but he doesn't budge.

"Tomorrow. Tonight stay here in my bed." He wiggles his hips and aligns our bodies.

"I shouldn't."

"I'll make you."

"How will you do that?"

He kisses my neck and I melt again. "Not fair."

"We have years of lost time to make up for. We've got tonight for that. Tomorrow you plan."

"Okay."

Chapter 17 The Haka

Mace

I'm powering into her and losing my mind as I finally bring her home. My hand is on her neck as she arches back, parts her lips, and struggles through desperate gasps before she moans, long and deep through her orgasm. The pulsing of her sweet pussy squeezing my dick sends me flying, and I'm incoherent, seeing stars, trying to savor it, but unable to focus on all of it at once.

I collapse on top of her in a sweaty, panting, sticky heap of flesh and hair. Best sex ever. Making love to this woman is absolute nirvana.

We're both smiling as the adrenaline zings unfettered, our hearts and bodies still shake with aftershocks.

"God, Mace. What are we doing?"

"We're fucking like monkeys." We've been up most of the night testing limits, exploring bodies, and rolling around on the floor like teenagers. "I'll let you rest five minutes then I got something else that'll rock your world."

She shakes her head from side to side. "No." She drags out the word. "I can't take any more."

"Okay. I'll give you ten minutes."

"Don't you have to teach a class or something? What did Sutton call it?"

"The Haka," I say quietly.

"Is it some kind of war dance?"

MEMORIZING MACE 171

I roll off her and look up at the ceiling. "No. Common misconception. It's used less rarely for war prep, more often for momentous events. It's a celebration of life."

She turns and rests her torso on top of mine, her hand under her chin.

"Have you ever been back to Hawaii? What island are you from?"

"Oahu. No. I haven't been back."

"Why not?"

"Haka is about family. My bio family in Hawaii abandoned me. I gave them up when I came here."

"How old were you?"

"Only two. I don't even remember my mom or dad. They signed away custody and never contacted me."

"Have you thought about contacting them?"

I sigh a long, heavy sigh and pull her closer. Lola asks all the hard questions. "I don't usually talk about it."

"I want to know."

"I thought about it when I was younger. I had this fantasy I'd go back to Oahu and become a surf legend. Now that I'm the big brother to so many other adopted kids, I don't want it. This is my family. I don't want to go pretend to love a stranger. I feel like it would disrespect my parents and dredge up a lot of old shit that can't be healed with words. I'm sure my bio parents just wanted what's best for me. I don't need to hear them say it or make them feel guilty for their decision. Does it matter if they know I'm happy now? Some of the kids have done it. It's not for me."

She stares up at me, waiting for me to continue, but I always land here whenever I get the idea of contacting my birth parents.

"Knowing you the way I do now, that makes sense to me. The past is inconsequential. We can't change it or talk it away. We move forward and enjoy today."

One more thing I like about Lola. She's a good listener. She's compassionate and caring.

"My grandfather was a true surfing legend. Can't top that. California waves are some of the best in the world. Now I'd be lying if I said I didn't want to surf in Hawaii, but I wouldn't want to go looking for my bio parents."

"I saw Henry's tree. I didn't know he was a surf legend."

"Yeah. There's a book about him and his wife. My dad has Henry's original copy of it. It's worn on the pages because it's been read so much."

"I'd love to see it."

I kiss her hard and pat her ass. "Later today I'll show it to you. We should probably get up for the haka practice now."

"Okay."

"Bar-b-que catered by Blackie's after, so you don't have to bring the fucking yams."

She slaps my chest. "Ha! Mila's face when her sweet little daughter blurted that out. I had to hold back from cracking up. So cute."

"She is cute. And she's probably waiting for us. We're ten minutes late already."

"We are?" She hops out of bed and starts looking for her clothes. I sit back and watch the show. She looks gorgeous naked. "Mace! I'm nervous enough about seeing your family again. I don't want to be late too. Let's go!"

I chuckle and haul my ass out of the bed to get dressed. "You're good for me, Lola."

"I am? How's that?"

"You wanna be on time for something, just get out of bed naked and run around. You'll have my full attention."

She chuckles and slips her bra on. "One thing."

"Hmm?"

"If you ever wanted to go back to Hawaii, I'd like to be there with you."

Her words punch me in the gut. She wants to be by my side if I face down those memories. "Thank you. That means a lot to me."

She blushes and looks away as she finishes getting dressed. I put on my karate uniform, and her eyes bug out when she sees me. She licks her lips and grins in a wicked way that makes me want to take my lioness back to bed right now.

We're both smiling as we make our way out the door to practice the haka with my family. Somehow, with just a few words, she made it mean so much more to me than it did before, and it was pretty damn important before.

I take her hand and squeeze it. "Glad you're here with me, Lola."

"I bet you are. You haven't had monkey sex like that ever before. Have you?"

My bark of laughter echoes out over the treetops. "No, I haven't. I've never met anyone like you."

Chapter 18 Hit Me

Loralei

Everyone is waiting for us by the boxing ring when we wander up. I'm struggling to hide my mortification at being late, but Mace's casual gait and easy-going smile make it seem like it's totally acceptable to walk up twenty minutes late to a class he's supposed to be teaching.

He keeps hold of my hand while he greets his dad with the Twist handshake, skipping the shoulder grab because his left hand is firm in mine. His dad doesn't say anything about us being late. He's probably used to it and too kind to nag Mace over it.

He gives his mom a more traditional hug and still keeps my hand tight in his. It's awkward but comforting that he wants to reassure me like he is. "Hi, Loralei. Glad you could make it." Mila has to be one of the nicest, prettiest moms I've ever met. How could I have hated this family so much before now? I know. It was jealousy. I'm lucky these people are so kind and forgiving they'd accept me here today.

"You're late, douchenozzle."

Clearly Cutter has no issues calling Mace out for who he is as he approaches us from the direction of the cabins. His arm is draped over Cass's shoulder, and I'm struck by what a handsome couple they make. She's petite and blonde. He has darker hair and is a lot taller, but they seem perfectly matched for each other.

"You're ugly. Just be glad I showed up at all. I coulda flaked on your ass leaving you all standing here waiting for me to arrive and save the day. Here I am." He finally lets go of my hand to raise up his arms and spin in a circle.

It makes me laugh, and Cass is smiling when she leaves Cutter's side to step over and greet me. "Hi, Loralei. How're you doing?" She seems genuinely concerned for me and touches my arm just above my elbow.

"Good. Excellent." I'm looking around the space for Sutton and Remy, but I don't see them. Maybe they decided not to come. I'd be so relieved to avoid that confrontation. It's selfish of me to feel that way though. I shouldn't wish for members of Mace's family to avoid coming home.

There was a time I would've loved to sow chaos for the Twists like that, but not now. Not anymore. These people are being so nice to me. I really don't deserve it.

Mace takes my hand again and leans down to whisper in my ear. "Relax. It's okay, my lioness. This is a safe place. Just be yourself."

I smile up at him, but I'm sure he sees the doubt all over my face.

"You are welcome here. Forget the past. The future has lots of monkey sex in it."

I'm blushing and laughing when he works his lips into the side of my neck and takes a playful bite. It's a simple thing but also a huge show of affection in front of his family. The tingling between my legs reminds me of how far Mace and I have come in a short time. It makes me feel like I can heal the wounds with his family too.

"Let's get started." Mace claps his hands, and everyone snaps into motion, jumping through the ropes, up into the square ring they use like a stage.

"C'mon. You can sit with me. We get front row seats." Cass takes my arm and guides us over to some chairs.

There's some confusion as they line up. "Should I save a spot for Remy?" Blaine asks.

"No. If he's late, he stands in the back," Mace replies.

This seems to answer a lot of questions because they fall into line quickly after that. Mace stands at the front facing them. He starts to talk about the haka and how they should put all their passion into every move. Cass leans over to whisper in my ear, "I remember meeting you here the night Jareth Quicksilver came up to cause trouble. We talked and you said Mace was more than nice, he was like a Hawaiian Jesus." She smiles like it was a fond memory.

"I said that?" Another wave of guilt crashes over me. I caused that fight. Nope. I'm forgiven. Not letting it get me down anymore.

"Yes. I remember laughing and thinking you pegged him exactly, and he's hard to describe in so few words. It was obvious you were crazy about him then."

"Was it?"

She nods. "Anyway, I'm happy for you it's working out with Mace."

"Thanks." Okay. These people need to stop being so nice to me, or I'm going to cry.

Luckily Mace is done talking to them, and he's turning around to face me. He grins like a naughty boy and winks as he strips off his shirt, flashing me with his gorgeous abs I've been worshipping for what feels like forever. My stomach flips. With his wink and partial striptease, a wave of renewed confidence washes over me. If he's brave enough to strip in front of his family, I should be strong enough to withstand a little humiliation, eat a little crow, and accept their forgiveness. He's right. I am welcome here. These are nice people, and they aren't holding grudges, so I should let go of the guilt. I have lots of wild monkey sex to look forward to. No need to sulk.

Mace barks out something tribal and savage. His family answers back with foot stomping and slapping their own bodies to make sounds.

Mace chants out a cry like an injured animal. They respond with a guttural grunt of affirmation. It's like he's calling out for help and they are saying, we are here for you. Mace's face grows dark and serious as the dance progresses, and his calls become more tortured.

Out of nowhere, someone charges the stage. My first instinct is to protect Mace, and I stand up. Then I realize the person is Remy. He barrels into Mace and knocks him down. We all watch in shocked horror as Mace and Remy wrestle on the mat.

Foster takes a step to intervene then stops himself. His face is tight with the effort. Mace throws Remy off and stands up. "You want a piece of this? Come get it." Mace challenges Remy with his arms out, chest heaving, eyes intense, and fingers curling inward. The Volcano has been activated, and he's beautifully terrifying.

Remy shakes his head imperceptibly. Not enough to be a firm no. He's breathing heavily too and staring at Mace like he's shocked at himself for rushing him. My heart thumps a frantic beat against my ribcage.

"C'mon. Hit me." Mace throws his arms back and puffs out his chest. "Hit me and let's be done with this."

Remy looks down at Sutton who also arrived as the haka started. She's standing on the ground at the side of the ring. She shakes her head no and trembles, but Remy turns his gaze back to Mace.

"Go ahead. Hit me. Then it's over. We never speak of it. Hard as you can. Right here." He smacks his abs with his palm flat.

Remy snarls and takes three short steps before punching Mace in the stomach. Mace heaves like he's about to vomit, his lips pressed tight together. Mila covers her mouth with her hands. Cass and Sutton look away. The guys are... laughing? I can't believe Remy just punched Mace in the stomach, and his brothers and his father think it's funny.

Remy opens his arms and offers his torso to Mace. Mace doesn't hesitate and socks him lower in the gut, where it has to hurt more. Remy doubles over and grips his stomach, but he's also gritting his teeth through a smile. "Ow, fucker."

Mace struggles to stand straight. "We good?"

Cass, Sutton, and Mila are giving in to the laughter too.

Is this a normal thing at the Twist residence? This is how they solve problems? By taking free shots at each other?

"We're good now." Remy hugs Mace, both of them chuckling and happy, patting each other on the back. I think I even hear a "Love ya, man" from Mace.

As weird as it seems to me, they obviously love each other, and the fight was their twisted way of showing it.

Sutton hops on the stage and wraps her arms around both of them. Something big has happened here, and I hope it means Mace and Remy can be brothers again like they were before I came into the picture. It looks like there's been some healing. I'm hopeful!

They break from their hug, and Mace motions with his hand for me to come up on the stage. I shake my head no.

He jumps over the rail, grabs my hand and awkwardly pulls me up onto the stage. His brilliant smile blinds me, and I'm still in shock when he plants a hot wet kiss on my lips that sends a surge of desire bounding up from my core. He dives into the kiss, tangling our tongues and releasing the horses from the gate. I have to stop him, or we'll end up doing the horizontal mambo right here in his family's boxing ring.

He grins and wipes his lip as he tugs my hips up against his body. "I told you everything would work out."

"I shouldn't have doubted the ways of Mace," I say somewhat jokingly. I didn't think fighting with Remy would solve anything, but apparently it has.

"Your face was so funny. You were truly scared."

"I was not."

"You worried I'd get hurt?"

No point in lying to him, he read it all on my face. "I was terrified. I felt like he was punching me in the gut."

He rubs his stomach in a circle. "No. That was definitely me."

"Are you okay?" I place my hand on his naked abs, and once again we're fighting off the sexual electricity between us. Can I touch this man anywhere and not get turned on?

"I'm fine. Gotta go finish the practice." He angles his head back toward the other members.

"Okay."

He kisses me one last time and releases me. My body cools as he puts some distance between us. I walk back to my chair and take a seat. Cass returns to sit next to me. "That was exciting."

I just laugh because it doesn't need to be said out loud.

My breathing returns to normal, and the adrenaline from the fight starts to wane in my system as the Twist Family returns to the haka formation. This time Remy and Sutton join the front row even though they are wearing street clothes and not a karate uniform. I have to smile seeing Mace and Remy chanting together, stomping their feet, and screaming loudly. A celebration of life and family, and I'm so lucky to be here to watch it.

***

After the practice, Mace held my hand and grinned as we waited in line for food from Blackie's. I received a delectable plate of bar-b-qued salmon, grilled veggies, and kale slaw and sat down next to Mace around the big stone fire pit near Mila and Foster's cabin. It was hard to focus on my food with a shirtless Mace glowing in the firelight and shedding his warmth all around. The man is truly comfortable in his own skin, and his joy is contagious. I found myself smiling too for no reason. It's just fun to be in his presence.

We clear our plates, and Mace takes my hand and guides me off into a shady corner behind his parents' cabin. I only catch a glimpse of the lake because he pins me against the wall and starts kissing me. His hands grip my hips and squeeze. "Let's resume the monkey sex."

"Everyone is here. We shouldn't leave."

"We made an appearance. No one will miss us. And if they do, screw 'em."

"You said you'd show me Henry's book."

Mace's attention is pulled back toward the bar-b-que. Cutter and Cass walk through the trees and stop next to us. Cutter's face is drawn, eyebrows pinched. The exact opposite of Mace's easy-going demeanor.

"We need to have a chat." Cutter levels his gaze on Mace.

"I was about to take Lola back to my cabin." Mace seems irritated.

"Don't brush this one off, Mace. We have to deal with it."

"Deal with what?" I ask.

"Does anyone else know you're here?" Cutter asks me instead of answering my question.

"No. I mean, except maybe Helix."

Cutter looks to Mace again. "You trust that guy?"

Mace shakes his head. "I have no idea. He hasn't done me wrong so far, but that doesn't mean the first time isn't waiting around the corner."

"We need to deal with the bounty on Loralei." Cutter wraps his arm around Cass and pulls her close. She looks worried and nods her head.

"I'm analyzing the data I collected on Diablo," I say, thinking this will appease Cutter. The more we know, the better. "I have a database."

Mace's arm around me tightens.

Cutter narrows his brow and squints at me. "A database won't keep you safe. There's a hit on you. If Helix gives away your location, we could be looking at an army of hitmen snooping around up here looking to take you out. Shit. There could be snipers watching us right now."

"I trust Helix and no one else knows I'm here."

"Diablo is not small-time and Giselle is running scared." Cutter's voice is bleak and alarming. "They both know you could provide the evidence that ties them to the murders."

"Shut up, Cut. Why don't you scream it a little louder? The squirrels on the other side of the lake didn't hear you." Mace's happy aura is gone, and he's tense again.

Foster and Mila walk around the corner and suddenly our little makeout spot in a shady spot is filled with big men and their women and they're all staring at me.

"What'd we miss?" Foster asks.

Cutter pops out one knee and turns toward Foster. "Mace isn't taking the bounty on Loralei seriously. She has some plan that involves data analysis, and an unreliable source possibly knows her location. So, not good."

"I'm taking it seriously," Mace snaps. "I'll handle it. I just got her back. All right? Give me a week to regroup, and then I'll go after Diablo."

"I don't think we have the luxury of a week to regroup, Mace." Foster sounds very father-like in the shadows like this.

"I'll take care of it myself."

"No," Foster replies.

"Mace, we can't let you face this alone." Mila is once again one of the nicest people I've ever met.

"We're in. This is too big for you alone," Cutter says. "Trust me, bro. I've been where you are and if you guys hadn't shown up, I'd be so screwed."

MEMORIZING MACE 183

"You handled Morganna without us," Mace reminds Cutter. "Can we take this somewhere a little less out in the open?"

Foster nods and turns away with Mila. "In the house."

Cutter and Cass follow them.

Mace leans down to kiss me once, but his lips are strained and hard now. "Sorry."

"They care about you, and they know now you care about me, so they want to help. I think we should hear them out."

He sighs and takes my hand as we walk out from behind the cabin, up the front steps, and enter Mila and Foster's living room.

Everyone is sitting on couches looking worried. Remy and Sutton walk in behind us. "What'd we miss?" Remy asks.

Mace rolls his eyes. "You've gotta be kidding me."

Cutter tells Remy the same things he told Foster. I don't like the way Cutter minimizes the importance of my data, but I'm used to controlling my ego when working with men. In the end, they always come to me for my data. They just don't see yet how it can help us.

Remy and Sutton take seats opposite us, and we all sit in silence for a moment. It is a dangerous situation, and we have to be careful how we approach this. "I go in as bait." The words blurt out of my mouth before I have a chance to process what it means.

"No." Mace replies instantly. "Nothing that puts you at risk."

"I'm at risk already. What're we gonna do? Wait for someone to show up here? Then we still don't have Diablo or Giselle. We get the middle man. We need to make them think they have me so they lead us to Diablo."

"No." Mace is louder this time, his jaw tight.

"You got another way to find Giselle? We're not even sure if we're looking for Giselle or Diablo or both. We'd have to have a two pronged approach to hunt them down." I don't like arguing with Mace in front of all these people, but he needs to agree so we can start planning.

"I don't like it. I want to hunt him alone," Mace growls. "Lola stays here. You guys watch her for me, and I'll get Diablo."

"What if Giselle put the hit on Loralei?" Cutter asks.

"Then I'll go after her next," Mace replies shortly.

"She is in the wind," Cutter says. "No one can find her. She has money and influence all over the world. She can get people to hide her anywhere. We have to act fast before she leaves the country."

"I understand why you're against it, Mace." Foster chimes in. "But it might be our only move at this time."

"We'll make sure she doesn't get hurt." Remy sits up straight and looks Mace in the eye.

Mace returns the look with a doubtful squint.

"We'll set Loralei up with tracking devices. Take every precaution." Cutter's voice is grave. He knows how serious this is, but I agree our only option is to be proactive.

Mace sits unmoving with his eyes on the floor. I place my hand on his bicep. "I'm an undercover cop, Mace. I know how to handle myself and how to execute an op like this. You need to have faith in me and your family right now."

"Faith." He huffs and shakes his head. "Fine," he says quietly. He lifts his gaze and narrows in on Cutter. "You make sure nothing happens to Lola. This guy already had her once and almost killed her. I don't like the idea of giving him a second chance."

"We know you don't like it, but it'll be worth it in the end when Diablo is off your tail, the bounty is gone, and you bring Loralei back here without having to worry about snipers in the trees."

He nods. "Okay."

"Good. Let's get to work."

***

Two days later, Mace ends a call with Helix. "He set it up for tomorrow at four pm. Still not comfortable with Helix doing the drop off." Mace runs his hands through his hair.

I look up from my laptop. "He's the only one who would legit do it. Anyone else and they'd suspect."

"He's a wildcard, and he'll be the one closest to you."

I stand up and walk over to Mace. "I think he's looking forward to proving his loyalty to you. I got to know him when I stayed at his place and trained with him. He's a good guy under the harsh surface."

Mace scoffs and doesn't smile. "I don't like the way it went down. You talk to him at Dragon Lounge, the same night you're getting explosives on your garage and cars running you off the road. Who else told them you were back?"

I raise one finger to stop him. "It wasn't Helix who spread the news I was back from the island."

"Who then?"

"Griffin. My ex."

"The creep who was looking in your window?"

"Yep. Right after you attacked him on my porch, he went and called Diablo. I couldn't believe it when I saw it in his phone records. Diablo made a bunch of calls after that. Probably organizing the explosives and the tail on me."

He props his hands on his hips and cocks one knee. "Your ex is involved with Diablo?"

"It looks like it. Apparently our fathers weren't only pedaling vitamins, they were dealing drugs. It pisses me off Griffin would betray me like that. Then he went and told Diablo I was looking for Hannah Clark and started this whole kidnapping-bounty nightmare."

A vein bubbles in his neck. "Where does this Griffin asshole live?" Uh oh. The Volcano is active again.

"No. Mace." I place my hand on his chest. "We're not going after Griffin. I'm only telling you this so you can trust Helix. He's not the one who betrayed me."

Mace stares at me and nods. "Fine. First Diablo, then Griffin."

I have to laugh at him. "They are not on the same magnitude at all. Diablo is a major drug trafficker. Griffin's just a druggie trying to get in good with him. Small fish. We need to focus on Diablo. What did Helix say?"

He stares over my head for a second as if the change in topic has scrambled his channels.

"On the phone just now? Where is the dropoff tomorrow?"

His gaze snaps to mine, and his eyes grow dark and serious. "Right. Okay. Ocean Beach Hotel. Good location. One main road into and out of the area. Water on the north side."

"Good. We need all the advantages we can get against Diablo. Or Giselle. Whoever we're dealing with here."

Mace reaches down and hauls me up against his body. "Not losing you. Not now."

"You won't lose me. And we'll get this cloud out from over our heads."

"It's not a cloud. It's a bounty."

"We'll get rid of that too."

He kisses me and drags me over to the bed. His kisses are desperate and urgent as he lays down on top of me. The mix of adrenaline and fear turbocharges my system. The anxiety rush is like an aphrodisiac. From the rigidness of Mace's body, he's nervous too but also getting off on the thrill. "I'm a bounty hunter now, Mace. You're gonna have to accept that I take risks like this."

He kisses down my neck. "No."

"Yes. It's who I am. I wouldn't ask you to change who you are."

He stills and looks up at me. "Right."

"So stop fighting it. Let's roll together. Let's be a team. An unstoppable duo."

He laughs.

"And with your family at our backs, what could go wrong?"

He doesn't answer. He continues to ravish me and take me to the edge of ecstasy several times before letting me feel the full force of it.

After the heat cools, and we're lying in bed together resting, I brace my arm on his chest and trace my fingertips through his hair above his ear. "I have a lot to live for now, Mace." It comes out as a whisper, but he didn't like it when I said I had nothing to lose. I want him to know I'm going to do everything I can to stay safe and return to this bed with him.

"Me too." His arm squeezes around my waist, and he smiles down at me.

Yep, definitely have a lot to live for now. Not letting my future with Mace slip away now that it's actually within my grasp.

Chapter 19 The Handoff

Mace

She's wired with the best and latest technology. Tracking devices in her purse and phone, and a small mic in her bra. He'd have to take off her clothes to find it, and there's no way I'm allowing it to go that far.

Her confidence is sexy as hell and not unfounded. She's a pro. I trust her. It's Helix and the unknowns that keep pinging my protective instincts and making me want to call this off.

Too late now. It's go time. I give her one last kiss and put all the things I can't say into it. She sighs and stares up at me with those eyes that always end with her naked. "I won't let anything happen to you."

She nods. "I know. Remember, if you need it, Sutton has access to the database on Diablo."

I wrap my hand around her neck and squeeze. "Okay." We don't even know if we're dealing with Diablo, and all the data in the world can't keep her safe, but I'm done fighting her on this. "Stay safe."

"Will do." I kiss her quickly and pat Helix on the shoulder harder than necessary. They walk out to the entrance of the Ocean Beach hotel while I listen in a rented van. Helix is wired with a hidden body cam but unarmed per their conditions. We're meeting a go-between here, and he'll take us to whoever placed the bounty. My money's on Diablo, but Cutter, who is in another car with Cass at the parking structure exit, thinks Giselle is behind this. She doesn't want to spend the rest of her life in prison, and Loralei is the only one of her victims who survived and is brave enough to talk. We'll find out soon enough.

Helix grips Lola's upper arm, and she pretends to resist as he forces her to the meeting spot. They approach the grand piano in the lobby of the Ocean Beach Hotel. No one is there yet, so they have to keep up their bickering act.

"I don't understand what this is all about. Why are we here?" Lola does an awesome petulant child routine.

"Shut up."

"Don't tell me to shut up. You brought me here against my will. I should call the cops." She crosses her arms and lifts her chin. She's doing well so far.

"Quiet."

About ten minutes into our wait, I'm starting to think our go-between—who said his name was Simon—won't show. I'm about to say something when a man with dark hair approaches them. He's wearing a slick black suit with a white dress shirt, unbuttoned at the top. He casually steps up next to Loralei.

"Simon?" Helix asks the go-between. It's probably not his real name, but it doesn't matter. He's not the man we're after.

"Excellent work, Helix." Simon eyes Loralei like a piece of meat, and I want to jump out of the van and pound that look off his face.

"Pay up." Helix raises his palm turned up.

Simon puts a hand on Loralei's arm. "The boss said you wait. As soon as I deliver her, he'll transfer the money into your account."

"How long will that be? I ain't got all night."

"An hour. The second I drop her off, you get the money. Can you wait sixty minutes?"

"You'd better not be blowin' smoke."

"You have my word."

Helix chuckles, and my gut tightens as the man tows Lola back toward the entrance to the lobby. She keeps up her struggling ruse. Simon stops, pulls a gun, and Lola flinches and whimpers as he stabs it into her back. "Stay put, Helix. Don't follow me."

Simon makes an unexpected turn toward a side door that leads to the parking structure. He forces her through it. My heart stutters as the door closes, and we lose our visual of Lola. She's alone with him, and we don't have eyes on her.

"Helix!"

"On it."

Helix's camera shows him opening the door and entering the parking structure. No Lola.

On her feed, we hear her and Simon's steps echo on concrete.

"Hey! What are you doing?" Lola's voice sounds panicked. "Don't touch me."

"Checking you for a wire."

Damn. Damn.

"Don't take my watch. Hey! That's my purse why did you throw that in the trash? That's my personal property."

The scuffle intensifies, and she's really fighting now.

"I can't listen to this," I say to no one in particular, but everyone is listening. We're all on this call and listening to Simon take off her mic and throw out her phone.

"She's okay, Mace. Trust her," my dad responds.

The thud from the speaker tells me he found her microphone and tossed it too. The last thing I hear is footsteps walking away and then nothing.

"No. We can't lose contact." I'm trying to rein it in, but I feel like screaming. "Helix, you got her in your line of sight?"

"I heard a door close," he says. "I'm heading that direction, but I don't see them."

"We need to watch the exits and track any cars that leave. Helix, watch the main exit and call out each car that leaves. We have to split up." My family and Wayne are stationed in separate vehicles around the hotel. We weren't supposed to split up, but we have no choice now. We don't know what car she's in.

Helix's camera shows a car leaving the structure. "Black Mercedes exiting right now."

"We'll take it," my dad says.

"White van came out of the delivery entrance," Wayne says. "I'm on it."

"Sutton..." I'm choking on the panic in my throat. This is chaos. It's falling apart. We've lost her.

"I'm here, Mace."

"I'm seeing red. I can't keep track of all these cars."

"We got it." She sounds calm and in control. "Mila and Foster are following a black Mercedes. Wayne is tracking a white van."

"We can only track six vehicles, max. What if they're in the seventh?" Shit. I'm losing it like a rookie. I feel like I'm ten years old again trying to pay attention in class, but everything is zipping around in a whirlwind.

"Helix will check any we can't follow. Blaine and Sequoia are on their way. Remy has his staff on standby if we need

MEMORIZING MACE 193

them." Sutton's voice reassures me. She's paying attention. She's following all the moving pieces for me and staying one step ahead. Thank God for Sutton.

"Black Tesla," Helix calls out. "Tinted windows."

"Cutter and Cass take the Tesla," Sutton replies.

"Got it." Cutter's voice. Also confident. Good. Cutter is good in situations like this. Unlike me who is bouncing all over the place.

God. I'm useless to her if I can't focus on something.

"Black Suburban exiting right now." Helix calls the next car as I see the front bumper pull out of the structure.

"Mace, you take the black Suburban," Sutton orders.

"What if..."

"You need one target. The black Suburban is your target. Don't worry about anything else."

"Got it." I take off following the Suburban and for a second, my brain cooperates, zooming in on the license plate number and calling it out for Sutton.

"Good, Mace. Remy, you're next," Sutton says, her voice shaking slightly, but she still sounds under control.

"Silver minivan coming out next." Helix keeps adding moving pieces to this chase. "Male driver. I stopped him, but couldn't see in the back of the van. Got a sketchy vibe from him, but no Simon. Worth a follow." He calls out the license number.

"I'm on the silver minivan," Remy replies.

Who's next? What's next? Fuck. My brain is all over the place. Where the hell is she?

"Helix, Blaine and Sequoia should be entering the parking structure right now."

"I see them."

Okay. I give up trying to follow what everyone else is doing. I'm on the Suburban. I trust my family to do their part.

"How long has it been since we've heard from her?" I ask Sutton.

"Fifteen minutes. My guess is they've left the structure already. They wouldn't sit in their vehicle knowing she was wired. They probably hit the road, especially if they're supposed to hand her off within an hour."

"Shit." The thought of Lola getting handed off to anyone without me there to protect her... "Fuck."

"Mace. You gotta keep it together. You're on the black Suburban. She could be in there. Everyone update your location."

My dad, Cutter, Remy, and Wayne call out their status, but I have to stay focused on my goal. "The black Suburban is heading up into Glen Canyon."

"It's not the Tesla." Cutter makes the call.

"Cutter and Cass, pull back and head out to meet Mace in Glen Canyon." Sutton is still in control and I'm still focused on my one target.

"No other cars have left the structure," Helix says. "We cased every inch. No one else in here right now."

"Position yourselves at each exit and be prepared to follow in a car." Sutton is doing a great job. Thank God for her skills because I couldn't do this alone.

Wayne eliminates the white van, and Remy gives another update.

The road forks, and I can't see the Suburban. I guess and turn right, but there's no sign of them. "I lost the Suburban. Fuck. This is so fucked up." I bang my fist on the steering wheel.

MEMORIZING MACE

I lost the one car I was supposed to follow. "If she gets hurt because of me..."

"We got 'em covered, Mace. We got 'em," Cutter says.

"We're spread all over the Bay Area and I just lost my target!"

"Where are you?" Sutton asks.

"O'Shaughnessy Boulevard. Glen Canyon."

Deep in my brain, I hear Lola's reminder about her data. "Sutton, check Loralei's intel for a residence in Glen Canyon associated with Diablo."

"Good idea. Stand by." Several tense moments pass. "Yes! Diablo ordered flowers delivered to a home in Glen Canyon. 1211 Congo Street."

"Got it." I program it into my GPS and make the turn. "I see the Suburban. Sutton, I love you."

"I love you too! Awesome."

Remy chimes in. "Not the silver minivan."

Sutton's voice ramps up when she replies. "Remy, get over to Glen Canyon ASAP. We're getting closer. I can feel it."

"It's not the Merc." My dad's voice confirms what I thought.

The Suburban pulls into the driveway of a house overlooking a steep canyon. It stops next to two other cars. "They're in the garage of the address Sutton gave us." Simon gets out of the driver's seat and walks around to open the passenger door. "There she is. Loralei just got out. She's fine. Not hurt. Hands not tied." I can't hide the relief in my voice. No more looking. We found her. "Simon is still with her." I can't tell if she still has a gun at her back. The garage closes, and I lose sight of them.

"I'm on my way," Remy replies.

The urge to run to her takes over. I can't wait for the others. She needs me now. "I'm moving in."

"Mace, wait. Wait for us to get there," Wayne warns. "We got her. We're on our way to back you up."

"I can't wait. I can't. I want her out now." I strain to see into the residence, but there's no movement. "I'm going in."

"Mace, wait," Wayne yells, but this isn't his gig. It's mine.

"If you want me to hold off, you need to get here in the next sixty seconds. After that, the volcano explodes, and it's game over."

"Wait for backup, Mace." Cutter's voice. "You helped me. Let me help you."

"I work alone."

"No. Mace. Not today." My dad's voice is the only one with a chance of reaching me when I'm like this. "We're your family. You don't get to make this choice. We're telling you to hold off till we're there. You have to trust Loralei on this."

I growl back at my dad. I can't argue with him. He's right. He's so right, and I hate it.

"Hurry the fuck up." It'll drive me insane, but I'll wait.

"We'll be there in a few minutes," Cutter says.

Okay. Cutter is close. I'll wait for him. He's good with a knife. I check my gun for the four millionth time. I don't need his knife. My gun will work just fine.

A car I haven't seen before pulls into the drive and parks in front of the garage door. My muscles spasm when Diablo of all fucking people gets out of the car. He approaches the front door casually like he's here to pick up a package. No way. He's not getting anywhere near her.

"Diablo's here."

I said I'd wait but that was before. This changes everything.

As he's taking the steps to the front door, I exit my vehicle and barrel toward him like a rabid dog who's been stuck in a cage his entire life and finally set free.

Diablo hears me coming and pulls a gun. He gets a shot off and misses. The momentum of my body hitting his throws us both to the ground and knocks the gun from his hand. I'm taller than him, but he's thick and starts throwing some loaded punches at me. I don't care if I get hurt as long as I can keep him away from Lola. Even better if I can distract Simon long enough for her to escape.

I hear a scuffle in the background, but I can't see what's happening. I'm too busy beating Diablo's ass.

Blood stains my knuckles and his face before Cutter finally shows up and stops me. He takes control of Diablo's arms and presses a knee to his back. "Where's Loralei?"

"Inside." Panting, sweating, heart pounding, I stand up and enter the house. Simon is passed out on the floor, and the place seems empty. Looking around, I catch a flash of brown hair flying out of a door. I follow her and see her jump into a Land Cruiser as it's pulling out of the garage.

Chapter 20 Hannah Clark

Loralei

Simon pokes me in the back with the barrel of his gun. So unnecessary. I'm not even fighting him.

I'm still angry he searched me and tossed all my tracking devices in the trash, but I'm not trying to get away. I don't want to escape Simon right now. I want him to lead me to whoever has this bounty on my head, so I can arrest them. We're in a luxury house up in the hills with the air conditioning blasting even though it's a cool day outside. I hope Mace and his family were able to follow us here. If not, I'm on my own.

Out of habit, I catalogue all the exits. Behind me, the front door, a big sliding glass door off the living room, and the inner garage door near the kitchen that we came through to get in. I remember noticing other cars in the garage, so there could be more people here. We stand silently and awkwardly in the living room. "Why are we here?"

Simon looks up. Giselle struts leisurely down the stairs like Norma Desmond in Sunset Boulevard. "Well, hello, Simon."

Ah, so it was Giselle. I would've bet money Diablo put the bounty out on me, but it was her. She must be very worried I'll spill everything I know, and she'll end up rotting in prison.

Seeing her triggers my memory again. Diablo dropped me off on the island. Introduced me to her. He kissed her. Diablo kissed Giselle. I get it now. They're a couple, and she was facilitating the transfer of women to Arthur.

I remember how she was so nice and welcoming to me, but then she offered me drugs. When I refused, she forced it on me.

She doesn't look like a bad person. She's dressed elegantly, like someone who has money. It's so hard to believe she's secretly trafficking women to transport drugs.

She reaches the bottom of the stairs and walks over to me. "Hello, Loralei." She fakes a smile and a sweet tone, but I see right through her act. "Or should I call you Leona?"

"Why am I here, Giselle?"

"I just wanted to speak with you."

"Here I am. Speak." I'm listening outside for any sign Mace has found me, but I don't hear anything.

"About the island. Well, people are trying to make it seem like I'm involved in some kind of drug operation, but I assure you I'm not."

She absolutely is. She's a fantastic liar. "Again, why am I here?"

Her gaze flicks over my shoulder to Simon. "I just need you to tell them you never saw me on the island."

She wants me to lie for her? "But I did see you, and you drugged me against my will."

Her eyebrows narrow. "Are you like your father?"

What? I'm shocked to hear her mention my dad. "What do you mean?"

"He was a goddamn self-righteous one too. Acting innocent when he wasn't. Accusing me of things." She leans back and props her wrists on her hips.

"If you mean am I going to tell the truth and get you arrested? Yes, then I'm exactly like my father."

Her face turns red. "That didn't work out so well for him. Did it?"

Oh. Now we're getting somewhere. "Were you involved in my father's death?"

"Of course not." She shakes her head and avoids my gaze.

"You were. You and Diablo are a team. You took out my dad for threatening to turn on you. Didn't you?"

"No." She feigns shock in her voice, but it's all clear now. These people took down my father, and now they want to take me out too. I need to get this guy off my back, so I can take her into custody, but he's not moving.

That's when I hear it.

A thump at the front door. Thank God. Is Mace here?

As we all turn to look, a shot rings out.

This is my chance. Approaching Simon from the rear, I slip my arm around his neck and pull him into a choke hold as I wrench him sideways. I push him off center and he falls. I jump one leg over his torso and stomp on his wrist until he drops the gun.

Giselle takes off running.

"Dammit."

I kick Simon in the balls as hard as I possibly can. He twists and grunts, but I still have his neck. I stomp on his balls with all my weight. He groans and doubles forward. He'll be hurting for a little while.

I leave him and chase after Giselle.

She has the garage door open, and she's backing a Land Cruiser out.

I run around to the passenger side and jump in just as the car is pulling away.

"Get out!" She pushes my shoulder.

I slam my door shut and put on my seatbelt as she looks out the back window.

Mace is running after the car.

She floors it, and we're off down the hill.

I punch her in the face. Her head snaps back and the car jerks. "Ow! That was uncalled for, Loralei."

"That was for Cass and Cutter."

She holds up a hand to block me, but she's trying to drive and she's an easy target now.

I punch her in the nose and hear a crack. "That's for Hannah Clark." She slams on the breaks, and the car starts spinning. I reach over to grip the wheel and hold it steady. I manage to grab the key and cut the engine. All I can do now is wait for us to slide to a stop.

Bushes crunch and tires skid before we finally come to a halt. I can't tell where we are, but the car is tipped at a steep angle.

Mace yanks my door open.

"Mace!"

His massive arm surges in and grabs my elbow. The car slips and I scream.

I hold onto his arm for dear life. "Don't let go, no matter what."

Mace wraps a strong arm around my waist and pulls hard. Once I'm out, I kick the frame of the car.

The Land Cruiser creaks. "That was for my dad."

The car slips and shakes.

The ground falls off below it.

The Land Cruiser tumbles down the steep cliff.

A blast knocks my eardrums, and the car bursts into flames. The dry brush around it ignites and a fire erupts.

Helicopter blades beat over our heads. Remy is watching from above.

Cass and Cutter come running down the street.

"Remy called 911," Cutter says.

We all stand around and watch the car burn.

Mace holds me tight in his arms.

I can't believe what just happened.

Sirens approach as he kisses me. "God. I hated that."

"It's okay. We're okay."

"Yeah."

Firemen and police arrive with sirens blaring, but I'm numb. They climb down the slope to put out the fire.

After twenty minutes, they pull her burned body from the Land Cruiser and cover it with a blanket.

Mace kisses me again. "I was so fucking worried."

"I didn't know if you guys were here."

"I was here. Cutter was right behind me."

"That was too close."

"You're okay now. You're safe."

Chapter 21 Shopping

Mace

A week after the ordeal with Diablo and Giselle, Lola continues to impress me. She handled all the fall-out like a pro. She had to interact with her counterparts at SFPD, and seeing her in her professional role for the first time confirmed what I already knew. Lola has a spine of steel. She doesn't crack under pressure, and she knows who she is. Her strong sense of justice guides her every decision, and she takes the law seriously, at least in front of her peers and superiors at the police department.

Lola ends the call with her captain and presses her lips together.

"What did she say?"

"Diablo's been transferred to the DEA." She speaks curtly and precisely, but emotion simmers in her eyes. She looks away when she senses me trying to read her.

"This is good news. He'll probably sing to get a reduced sentence. You've done a good thing." She's shown no sign of guilt or regret for sending Diablo to prison or Giselle to visit the devil, so why is she hesitating now? Delayed reaction?

"I'm going shopping." Her knuckles turn white as she rubs her hands together.

"Okay." I stand up and grab my keys.

"What're you doing?" She stares at my keys in my hand.

"I'll take you."

"It's just shopping. I can do it alone. You'll be bored."

"Babe. You just got off the phone with SFPD, a vein is popping in your temple, and your voice is strung out. I'm coming with you on your shopping trip."

She looks around like she's misplaced something. "Um. Okay."

All this is suspicious from a woman I'd trust with my life. "You gonna tell me what this is really about?"

She jets around the room, grabbing her shoes, a purse, a jacket and stumbles to the door. "Right now I'm going shopping. That's all I can tell you. If you're coming, let's go. I'll drive."

"I'm driving."

"I need to *drive*." She spins and growls at me like a caged lion. "I need to drive my Maserati. Fast. If you're coming, be prepared to buckle in and shut up."

I chuckle and push my keys into the pocket of my jeans. I walk over to her and kiss her temple, but she remains stiff. "If you need to work off something, we can do that right here without breaking the speed limit. I'm fully able and willing to let you take this out on me." I raise my arms and look down my body.

Her gaze follows mine down to my shoes. On the way back up, she stops to stare at my junk, her eyes turning hot. Her tongue juts out and swipes her lower lip, but her shoulders are still up to her ears. "Later." She shakes her head to break the hypnotic power of my dick through my pants. "Right now I need to drive and go shopping. Then I'll take it out on you."

I have to laugh at how she's making elaborate plans to deal with whatever's stressing her out instead of just doing what feels right to get it out. "We could fix this all right now with a good hour in my bed, but if you need to shop and drive first, I'm okay with that."

"You're confusing me, Mace."

"You're overthinking this."

"No. No. Because if we stop and have sex right now, I'll still need to go shopping afterward. It won't fix this. So shopping, driving, then monkey sex."

"Sounds like a plan." I smile and wrap an arm around her waist as we walk out of my cabin. "Whatever you need, my love."

She gasps and looks up at me. That's the first time the L word has come out of my mouth around her. I just grin down at her. I said it. Deal with it. She's going to be hearing a lot more about love from me very soon, so she'd better get used to it.

***

After a hair-raising cruise in the Maserati, we end up parked in front of Fantasy Island Adult Gifts in Sacramento. "A sex shop?"

"Yep. This is perfect."

"We buying toys?" We haven't used any toys in the bedroom yet, but if she wants to, I'm open to it.

"One toy. A dildo."

Uh. Maybe I'm not open to that. "If you're looking for a dick up your ass, I'd be happy to provide one."

"This isn't about one dick, Mace." She pulls the key out of the ignition and opens her door. "It's about a lot of dicks."

She closes the door and marches into the store. I watch her from the car and laugh. I have no idea what she's up to, but she has my full attention.

***

Two stops later and her backseat is loaded up with dildos of all sizes and colors, plastic wrap, and glitter. She still won't tell me what she's up to, but I'm laughing my ass off as we drive out to San Mateo.

"You wanna tell me who we're getting revenge on?"

She stops in front of a two-story condo at the top of a hill. "Griffin."

"Ahh." Her ex who had ties to Diablo. "I thought you said he was small fish?"

"That was before he cost me my job."

She reaches into the backseat and grabs handfuls of her supplies.

"He cost you your job?"

We both close our doors and talk over the top of the car.

"My supervisor just laid me off. Permanently. No more uncertainty. All because stupid Griffin told Diablo I was back. He set off the chain of events that led to the bounty on me and Giselle falling to her death. And the end of my career as a cop."

"I see."

"So now he pays." She marches toward the front door and I follow her.

"I have to say I like your ire so much more when it's not directed at me."

She plops her bags down on the porch and starts duct taping dildos to the front door. I sit back and watch her do her work. A big pink one on the door handle itself has me beaming.

The plastic wrap is weaved between them and anchored to a post. She works quickly with determination. There's no humor for her in this. I'm laughing my ass off watching her take this so seriously.

"Almost done."

The final step is glue and rainbow glitter all over everything she just created. No one is going through that door without getting glittered. I have to laugh remembering when she did this to my truck. I had that shit in my hair and fingernails for days.

She takes a step back to admire her work. "It'll do." She turns and marches back to the car with her empty bags.

I get in and smile at her. "We done?"

"One last thing." She picks up her phone and presses the screen. "Hi, Captain Sanchez. This is Loralei Valentine. I want to add to my report one of Diablo's dealers." She says the address twice. "I'm sure you'll find plenty of evidence inside that residence." She ends the call and looks at me. For the first time since the call with her supervisor, she's smiling. "Done."

I wrap my hand around the back of her head and pull her in for a kiss. "You are diabolical."

"A little revenge on the former employer at the same time doesn't hurt."

"Are we gonna stake it out and watch?"

"Nope." She wipes her hands together like she'd dusting off the last of the glitter. "I don't need to watch. I'm good."

I kiss her again and laugh. "Let's go to the bluffs."

"The bluffs? Why?"

"Let's go tell your dad Diablo is in jail, Giselle is in hell, and Griffin will pay in glitter."

She giggles and starts up the car. "All right."

***

The wind of the bay pushes her hair back and whips it around her face. I'm sitting on the hood of the car near the front driver's side tire, my legs spread, Lola between them looking hesitant again after her display of unfettered mojo earlier.

I run my thumb over her cheek. Her skin is cold, so I place my palm there to warm her up. I wrap my arms around her and hold her to my chest. "Tell your dad."

"No. It's silly."

"Tell your dad what happened today or I will."

She purses her lips and shakes her head.

"All right. Hey, Emrick. This is Mace!" I call it out into the wind like he's standing at the edge of the bluffs. She giggles. "Your daughter here is badass."

She pushes on my chest. "Shut up."

"Your girl took down a drug lord, a human trafficker, and a dealer all in one week."

"His girl also lost her job. The career she's given up everything for since he died. It was all I had. I was trying to prove..."

"What were you trying to prove?"

"I don't know. That he wasn't a bad guy. That I'm not like him. Redeem the Valentine name. God, it sounds stupid to say it, but getting fired from my job makes me feel like a failure. I can hear the gossip at work. *She's like her father. Bad to the core.* Giselle said it too. She asked me if I'm like my father. She called him self-righteous."

"And now she's dead."

"I didn't intend to kill her." Her voice is strained because she's had a long week of talking to investigators to convince them she didn't murder Giselle. No one told them about her last kick of the car before it went over the edge. That's a secret between us.

"Do you really want to spend the rest of your life trying to prove your father was good or that you're not out there repeating the parts of him that went bad?"

"No. It's exhausting."

"Exactly. You know people say I'm a tumbleweed made of razor blades."

"That's not true."

"Isn't it? Don't I blow through someone's life, take away someone they love, destroy their life like I did yours?"

"No, because sometimes it's better if that person faced justice instead of continuing to get away with hurting people and bending the law to their will."

"Who am I to judge that? It messed up your life. If I hadn't taken your dad in..."

"My dad bought and sold drugs. He abandoned those kids. It was right what you did."

"It's complicated. I admire what you're doing for your half siblings. Not many people out there would do that."

"I guess that's part of trying to prove I'm not like him."

"Do you go visit them?"

"Not as often as I should. I get busy with work."

"Wouldn't that be the best way to prove you're not like him, by not abandoning them?"

"I haven't abandoned them. I send money regularly."

"Don't you think they'd like to spend time with their half-sister who obviously cares about them? Where do they live?"

"Southern California. Santa Ana."

"I have an idea."

"Uh oh. What idea, Mace?"

"Nothing."

"Tell me."

"We fly down, bring Maisey and Henry, we pick up your siblings. How old are they?"

"They're seven, eight, and ten. Two girls and a boy. But this is an elaborate idea."

"It's forming in my head. We take them to Disneyland. Call their mother. See if they can go this Saturday."

"I don't know."

"Listen. I'm making plans. That is a rare event. I like this idea. We're doing it. You'll see. You'll have so much fun." I rub my hands together and laugh at her reservations. "You haven't been before. You don't know why they call it the happiest place on Earth."

"No. I don't, but..."

"So, you need to find out. This is important. We'll go this weekend."

She shakes her head. "You're crazy."

I take her cheeks between my palms, and she looks up at me with those eyes that say she trusts me to take her to new places, even when she's worried. "I'm crazy in love with you."

"What?" Her eyes flare and brighten.

"I love you and everything about you." The words have never come out of my mouth before, but right now it feels like the most absolutely truthful thing I could say to her.

Her chest is heaving and she's gasping for air like she just ran a mile. "I love you too. I think I always have."

"Good." We seal the deal with a hot tender kiss on the bluff, with her father looking down on us. There's one more thing I need to tell her.

"I know of a job opening you might be interested in."

"You do? I can't be a cop anywhere now. No one will hire me with my baggage."

"Not a cop position."

"What is it?"

"It's a bounty hunter position with a privately owned small company."

"Oh, is it now?" She smirks up at me and squeezes me in a hug.

"The CEO heard Leona Hart is the hot new thing coming up the ranks. He wants her on his team. Bad."

"Oh, does he now? Could he possibly be the amazingly gorgeous bounty hunter every girl has at the top of her bucket list?"

I chuckle and hold her tight. "You know the joke about the bucket-list brothers?"

"Oh, it's no joke. It's like a life board topper for all the girls in town. They're all chomping at the bit to land the drop-dead gorgeous, brave, and strong Hawaiian Jesus."

I pull her closer and she falls on top of me. "Really want to fuck you on the hood of this car."

She gasps. "Me too."

We work it out with our clothes so I can sink my hard dick into her scorching heat. It's not easy, but it's fantastic. She releases the lion and growls as she comes hard. I follow her over and press my forehead into her neck as we catch our breath.

Mace and Loralei. A team meant to be.

I guess even a tumbleweed made of razor blades can find its match.

Chapter 22 Roller Coaster

Loralei

Mace followed through on his plan. It took a few weeks to find a day all the kids had off school and sports, but Mace handled all the details. Watching Mister Spontaneous try to plan ahead was funny, but he pulled it off. We flew with Remy and Sutton, Cutter and Cass, and Maisey and Henry down to Santa Ana to pick up a van and my three half-siblings.

When we got there, I was shocked to see Mila and Foster plus Mace's other younger siblings; Blaine, Sequoia, Harley, and Marshawn.

I hug Mila and laugh. "What are you guys doing here?"

"We didn't want to miss out on the fun."

Mace pays for all the tickets. We could have bought a small car with the fee, but he's smiling as he puts his wallet in his back pocket.

As we wait in line for Star Tours, Mace totally geeks out. "Did you hear about the Wookie cookie?"

"No. What?"

"It's a little Chewy."

"Oh my gosh. That's awful." I smack him in the stomach and hug him. His inner child is very happy at Disneyland and he looks incredible in his jeans with a chain hanging from the hip and a torn T-shirt. I like watching him walk with the kids, towering over them with his heavy gait like a casual Godzilla.

After the ride, which was totally exhilarating and fun, he takes the whole group to the roller coaster in the park next to this one. It's a long walk, and we passed a bunch of attractions on the way, but he insists we have to do the roller coaster next.

He's smirking as we get into the front carriage and our family files in behind us.

"We got the front seat!"

He twists his lips and stifles a laugh. Something is off with him. He's extra goofy today.

His hand grabs mine as the old-fashioned wooden coaster clicks and gravity tries to tug us down to the ground, but we're climbing high. "I love you, Lola."

"I love you too, Mace." Odd time for him to say it, but I never get tired of hearing it.

"I want to ride the roller coaster of life with you."

That makes me chuckle. "Okay."

We're climbing higher and the view is fantastic. The warm breeze brushes my cheeks as we look down on Disneyland and Southern California. I'm so incredibly lucky to be here today with this amazing man and both of our families. We've been through some losses and challenges to get here, but it's all worth this moment right now.

We're about to crest the top and the clicking slows, my belly flip-flops in eager anticipation of the fall to come.

"Lola?"

"Yeah?" When I look at him, his eyes are misty and his smile lights up his face.

"Marry me."

"What?"

"Hurry and say yes before we go over the edge."

Oh my God. He wants to... He brought me here? Oh my God.

Gravity is wreaking havoc in my ribs as we crest the top. *Click. Click. Click.*

This is it. We're about to go crashing down and spinning out of control.

And I love it.

"Yes!" I manage to blurt it out as the wind whooshes past my ears. We're in freefall. My heart leaps up into my throat, and forces my mouth open. I have no choice but to scream at the top of my lungs. "Yes!"

He's smiling and laughing as the coaster thrashes us from side to side, twisting and turning and threatening to drop us over the edge.

"Awesome."

After another out-of-my-mind two minutes, the ride comes to a stop and we're both high and happy as we exit the carriage. He's still holding my hand when he drops down on the platform.

On one knee!

He pulls a ring box from his jacket pocket and opens it for me. A gorgeous pear-shaped diamond sparkles up at me.

"Be mine forever, Lola."

"Oh my God. That's..."

My throat clogs and my heart explodes. I get to be with this sexy, beautiful, brilliant, imperfect person for the rest of my life.

He puts the ring on my finger and I can barely speak. He stands and lifts me up to my tiptoes as he kisses me. Our families and everyone on the platform clap, including the employees. The kiss is deep and hot and wet.

"You surprised me," I say after the kiss.

"Be ready for lots of surprises if you're gonna marry me."

"I can't wait."

"You're going to be Mrs. Mason Twist."

"There's no one else I'd rather be."

***

"I sent out the invitations today." I drop it casually when it's anything but casual.

Mace and I are in bed, cuddling side-by-side after an early morning round of who can tease who the longest. He won. This is the best time to talk to him because he's open, his mind is focused, and he's too worn out to fight me on anything.

"Mmm?"

I pick up the square invitation with vibrant purple orchids and tea leaves decorating the edges. He glances up at it then does a double take as his eyes widen. His pupils read the lettering and his mouth drops slowly open.

His gaze turns to mine, and he looks like a boy who's just caught Santa kissing Mommy under the mistletoe. "You sent these out?"

"Yep. It's a done deal. No changes. It's a small guest list. Most of them live right here."

"Lola." He smashes his palm to his forehead. "I cannot believe you did that."

"What? You said you haven't been to Hawaii because your family is here. Your family will be in Hawaii when we get married there."

His arm snakes out and circles my waist. He smirks and tugs me up onto his chest. "We're getting married in Hawaii?"

"Yep. It's time for you to go. The waves are calling you. Your family and I will stand by your side as you face down your memories. Then we'll all go surfing."

He lifts his head to kiss me and smiles through the kiss. "I love you, my lioness."

"I love you too, Volcano."

He chuckles.

***

On the bluffs of Oahu, overlooking a pristine Hawaiian sea, Mace and I hold hands as our families form an arch around us. The wind whips our hair and clothes and random papers and napkins fly over the cliff, drawing a chuckle from the guests. Mace looks stunning in his ecru linen suit with an embroidered white dress shirt, open at the collar. I found a dress that looks better than leather pants on me. The sleeves fall slightly off the shoulder and the long mermaid train swishes behind me. You can't tell at first glance, but the lace is leopard print. Mace loves it.

Per his wishes, we didn't invite his biological father or anyone from his Hawaiian family. The Twists have a rule that you don't bring your past up the mountain, so he didn't want it up on this bluff today. He only wanted the people who love him unconditionally and allow him to love them back.

Cutter looks gorgeous at Mace's side as his best man. Cass glows in a flowy pastel-pink maid-of-honor dress. Wayne is performing the ceremony, and everyone smiles as he tells embarrassing jokes about Mace. In my head, my dad looks down on us and gives us his blessing. He'd be proud I tossed my life board and followed my heart. And he'd be happy I stopped trying to prove myself to everyone else. When the love around you makes you confident, you don't need to prove it to anyone else, you're too busy enjoying it and savoring each moment.

Wayne glances to the back of the rows of guests. Mace and I both look. Helix walks in late, shoulders hunched forward, head down, and sits in the back row. He's trying to look inconspicuous, but he's a tall man wearing a retro gray suit that stands out against the blue Oahu sky. Mace raises his eyebrows at me, and I smile. I told him I'd invited Helix, but I didn't expect him to come. The invitation was a sign of goodwill that we trust him after all that happened. Besides, he looks like someone who needs to be part of something else, so he's a welcome part of our wedding. He's our friend.

Mace and I return to our vows and promise to love, honor, and cherish each other through sickness and health all the days of our lives. Mace's knee bobs and his fingers squeeze mine as Wayne pronounces us husband and wife. He hoots and picks me up, swirling around as we kiss. Never in a million years could I have dreamed of being so happy, so in love, and so totally excited about the road ahead. With Mace by my side, it's going to be a glorious ride.

Chapter 23 Seger

Mace

"Hey, yeah, I'm driving around your neighborhood. I have a package for... James Acosta, but the address is wrong."

"You got a package for James?" The voice on the other end of the line is cautious.

"Yeah. I need a signature. Can I get the correct address?"

"Who's it from?"

"It's a package from Virginia Acosta. Looks like a birthday gift?"

"Yeah. Um. I'll sign for it. Bring it to 20145 Greenbriar."

"Thanks, man."

I end the call and smile at Lola. "Got him."

"Did he say James is there?"

"No. But I think that was him I was talking to. He was pretending to be someone else. He wants his package from his mom."

She nods and smiles.

We pull up to the address the skip gave us and scope it out. It's a trailer in downtown Stockton. It's run down as hell, broken windows, weeds growing up through the porch. One story.

"That's his car." She points to a rusted red sedan in the driveway.

Lola straps on her vest and checks her weapons. She's wearing her fugitive recovery badge and a black shirt that says "Agent" down the sleeves. We'll take tasers and pistols.

"Be careful, baby."

"No problem. Let's get this loser."

This asshole was arrested for abusing his kid and skipping out on child support. He was released on bail and failed to appear in court. This is exactly the kind of scumbag I love to bring to justice.

Lola loves it too. She's got her game face on and her eyes are lit. She's sexy when she's ready to whoop some ass. I lean in and give her a kiss. We exit the car and approach the house with me taking the front position.

She goes around the back and peeks in the windows. She holds up a finger. One person inside. Excellent.

The door feels paper thin when I knock on it. I could easily kick this thing in. We'll give him a chance to open it first. "Delivery."

When he doesn't answer, it's time to let him know what's up. "Fugitive recovery agents. Open up."

I hear some movement in the house and the kitchen window opens. He throws an empty bottle of Jack Daniels at me. It misses.

"You throwing shit at me, asshole?"

Oh I love it when they fight. The energy between Lola and I hits the roof. We're both on full alert now. He could run. He could have a weapon. We have to be smart. "Open the door, James, or I'm kicking it down."

"Fuck you," he replies and tosses some trash out the window at me. If he's throwing papers, it's pretty safe to assume he doesn't have a weapon. I give her the signal to enter from the back. A quick kick at the knob level and the door swings open and ricochets back so I have to kick it again.

He's standing in the hallway between the front room and bedroom. There's one closed bedroom door next to him. He's dirty and his hair is oily. His pupils are dilated and he matches the picture. It's him.

"You're coming with me, James. Got some warrants out for your arrest." I take a step toward him. He's unarmed.

"No. I don't got no warrants."

"You do. Beating the crap out of a little kid? Not paying child support? Any of that ring a bell?"

Lola steps into the hallway from the back entrance. His hands shake. He has no way out.

He pushes the bedroom door open and rushes inside. He tries to get the window open, but he can't. He reaches down and grabs... a baby by the arm. The baby cries out. His long curly hair hangs in his eyes. His dark skin is filthy and only a pair of thin shorts covers him. He looks exactly like me when I was a baby.

The day Wayne came in and arrested my dad, I was almost exactly the same age.

James's grimy hands grab the kid by the neck. "I'll kill him."

I'm frozen solid. Seeing that kid. I can't move. If I move, I'll kill a man. If I move, I'll pull my gun and start shooting and I could hurt that kid.

Lola steps up behind me. She gasps when she sees the child.

When I don't respond, she takes over. "Is that your child, James?"

"Bitch said it's mine and left it with me. I don't know for sure. Gonna get a DNA test but it cries all the fucking time. I hope it's not mine."

The baby wails and it pierces my ear like I'm standing in front of a siren.

My hands ball into tight fists. I can barely hold back. Lola places one hand on my arm to steady me. She knows the day Wayne saved me was the most important day of my life. She knows everything I do stems from that day. Everything I do is making sure that kids who need to be saved have a hero. Because nothing is worse than being stuck in hell and no one comes to save you. It just takes that one person to care and make a difference.

"Put the baby down." Lola speaks for me because I'm still locked up.

James holds the kid like a football and uses his other hand to mess with the window lock. "Stay back."

"You're not going anywhere. Put the baby down." Lola points her taser at the guy.

She won't shoot while he's holding the kid, but she's trying to scare him. White hot rage erupts in my chest. He's using a baby as a shield? What kind of asshole does that? The kind of asshole that beats his kids, doesn't pay child support, and doesn't show up for a court date. It's an innocent baby stuck in the mess of his father's chaos.

"Put the baby down right now or you're getting shot," Lola says. She's keeping her cool, but her muscles are strung tight and her voice is strained.

"I'll kill the kid."

That snaps me out of my haze, and I whisper quickly to Lola, "I'll nail him, and you take the baby."

She nods.

I shoot his leg, and he doubles over in pain. Lola grabs the baby and runs out. My fist connects with his face, and the crunch of his bones feels awesome. "You never ever ever use a child like a shield. Who the fuck are you treating a defenseless kid like that?" I can't stop pounding his face. He's bleeding now, and I don't care. He passes out, but I can't stop pummeling this bastard. He needs to die.

"Mace! Stop."

"I can't."

"Stop. You'll kill him."

She tugs on my bicep and almost catches my elbow as I'm winding up.

"It's not him. He's not your dad. Stop. He's a stranger. You'll go to jail for killing him. You have to stop. For me."

It's the "for me" that penetrates my crazed mind. For her, I'd do anything. For her, I can stop.

I raise my fists and back away from him.

Lola is holding the baby.

We're both panting and trying to catch our breath. The baby has stopped crying but his eyes are wet and frightened.

"What do we do now?" she asks.

If my brain was locked up before, it's crystal clear now. We have two choices. "We could call the cops and deal with the fall out."

"Or?" Her tone makes it clear she's hoping for a better alternative.

"Or we take that baby and get out of here."

She looks around the place and bites her lip. "What did Wayne do?"

"He took me and ran."

Her mouth drops open and her face pales. "That would be kidnapping."

"James doesn't know who we are. No one knows we were here. We take the kid and go."

"What about him?" She points at James, who appears to be alive, but still unconscious on the floor.

When I look at him, I want to beat him more. My lips curl up over my teeth. "Don't give a shit."

"What about the bounty?" Her voice rises. She's panicking, but I'm getting more confident with this decision every minute.

"We'll call Helix. He can clean this up. He won't know about the kid."

"Are you sure?"

My brain worked through this scenario fast. There's only one choice. "I'm not leaving that kid here or turning him over to the authorities. He said the mother abandoned him. We need to help him."

The baby has stopped crying and is looking from her to me like he's listening.

"Let's go. We'll call Helix from the car."

We exit the house and she sits in the back of the car with the baby on her lap. "Are we really doing this?" She cradles his head in her palm.

"We are."

I start the car and tear out of the driveway.

"Goodbye, James. You'll never see this kid again."

***

The farther away from James's house we get, the more Lola relaxes. The baby falls asleep on her chest. She's still holding his head in one hand, his bottom in the other.

Her head bobs and falls down. She's crying.

I get what she's feeling. That poor baby was in a room in that house for God knows how long. The father was a violent criminal who would use the child and put him in danger. It feels like we got there just in time to save him.

"I was about his age when Wayne rescued me."

"I know." She wipes a tear from her cheek. "I felt everything you were feeling. We're so in tune with each other, I was feeling all your pain. I saw you as a baby in his sweet little eyes. I felt his cries like they were yours."

I didn't realize that's what was happening at the time, but now it makes sense. "Yeah. It was intense. It knocked me off kilter. I was frozen trying to process it."

"It was heavy. It still is. He's such a sweet baby. He's sleeping in my arms, but we don't have anything for him. No car seat. We need formula and diapers. He looks old enough to eat solid food. We don't know his name or his birthday."

"We might be able to find his birth records."

"He's so precious. He's an innocent child. He doesn't deserve any of that. He needs love."

"Yep." I feel it in my bones. She's crying for him and me at the same time. We need love.

"We should really bring him to the authorities. We can't steal him, but we couldn't leave him there."

She's second guessing it, but I'm sure we made the right decision. "Let's talk to my parents when we get home. They know more about the system and what the options are. For tonight, we have to take him. He needs care. We'll bring him home, make sure he's healthy, and then we'll figure out what to do."

"Okay. Thank you, Mace. I love you." She sniffles and lowers her head again.

"Love you, Lola. With all my heart forever. No matter what."

Chapter 24 Epilogue

Three years later
Loralei

Mace leads the haka with his little man, Seger, at his side. Foster and Cutter are up there with all the Twist siblings. Mila and Cass sit next to me looking up at their men.

"You're not doing the haka today?" Mila asks me.

"I decided to sit out today. A little tired."

"I'm kinda glad I'm pregnant because I like to watch," Cass replies and raises her eyebrows as she ogles Cutter with his shirt off. He's covered in a mosaic of scars and tattoos that make him look dangerous and sexy. "Oh my God, Seger is so cute." She claps her hands.

"He's ours for good. Free and clear." They know the news already, but it's the first time I've seen them since Mace told them.

Mila and Foster were able to call in some favors with the local adoption agencies. James signed his parental rights over and Seger became our son officially a week ago.

"I'm so happy for you." Mila gives me a big hug.

Cass reaches over to embrace me too. Her pregnant belly bumps into my stomach. "You're going to have two new little Twists up there doing the haka with Uncle Mace soon."

"Not too soon. I have to pop these babies out first then get them walking, but I'm sure Cutter will have them doing karate in their little diapers."

We sit and watch the family finish up the haka. Four-year old Seger is Mace's little dude. Mace likes to tell me I'm the fuel in the engine of our little family, but it's not true. Seger and Mace are huge contributors to the happiness we're enjoying. Mace's never ending optimism and zeal for life keep us all motivated and excited for every day.

"I thought I loved Mace when we said our vows, but I didn't know then I'd love him as much as I do now. How did I get so lucky?"

"I feel that way about Foster. It just gets stronger every day as we get to know each other more deeply." Mila grins, and you can see the love glowing in her eyes.

"Me too! The more I know Cutter, the more I love him." Cass smiles up at Cutter on the stage.

"And they look hot in those karate pants," I say.

"Well, they are my sons, but I agree they are shockingly gorgeous."

My stomach gurgles, but I'm not hungry. "I feel like crap and my boobs hurt."

Their heads turn slowly toward me. "Are you pregnant?" Mila asks.

"No."

"How do you know?" Cass asks.

"I'm not late for my... Well, um, I might be a little late. But I'm taking the pill."

"The pill isn't one hundred percent. Ask me how I know." Mila glances up at Henry and Maisey on the stage.

"We were trying, but I felt tired and my boobs hurt before the test came back positive." Cass's voice is really excited.

"Leave it to Mace to get me pregnant while I'm on birth control."

"His super swimmers are probably turbo charged," Cass says. "Just like him."

"Oh my God. Do you think so?"

"Let's go check." Cass grabs my hand. "I have plenty of leftover tests."

Mila follows us inside Cass and Cutter's cabin. Cass hands me a pregnancy test from under the sink in her bathroom. "Pee on the stick, girl."

"You really think?"

"Can't hurt. Pee on it."

"I don't even know how. I've never done this."

"Just hold it in the urine stream for a second. It's not hard."

"Okay."

My hands shake as I squat over the toilet and pee on the stick.

"Oh shit. Holy shit. Cass!" Mila grabs the stick.

"What?"

"It's making a blue plus sign!" She shows me the results window as I'm buckling up my jeans.

Mila hands me the stick.

"You are knocked up, girl," Cass says.

"Oh my God." Tears well in my eyes. "I can't believe it. Are these things accurate?"

"Pretty accurate," Mila says.

Cass nods. "I had a dark plus sign like that too. Girl, we're going to be pregnant together." She smiles and her eyes light up.

I'm staring at her when Mace comes in. "What's going on?"

He looks so handsome with a layer of sweat glistening on his chest.

I hide the test behind my back, but his eyes track it. He takes three steps toward me and kisses me. He tastes like man and pure Mace. Just his kiss gets me turned on, and I want to jump his bones. He's amped up from doing the haka and grunts and deepens the kiss.

His hand grabs the stick out of mine as he breaks the kiss. He stares at it. Mila and Cass are pressing their lips tight trying to hold in their excitement. I'm still in shock. I can't believe it.

"Is this?" His voice breaks, and his eyes light up.

I nod and smile.

"You're gonna have my baby?" The emotion in his voice pierces my soul. This means everything to him.

"According to the stick, yes!"

"Woot!" He slugs the air like he just won a big fight. "Damn! We did it?"

"And we weren't even trying!"

"My God, woman. You just made me the happiest man on Earth, and I was already the fucking happiest man on Earth."

"You want this?"

He leans down and looks me in the eye. "I want this. I want you. I want us. Forever. Best fucking news ever. Imagine a little girl as pretty and sweet as you."

"Imagine a boy, handsome and strong, like you."

His beaming smile widens. Seeing him like this is everything. I want to give him joy like this all the time.

He bends down and scoops me up by my ass. My hands fall to his shoulders. "Mace!"

He marches out of Cass's cabin and back to the firepit. "Hey, everybody!"

Oh no. Please don't.

MEMORIZING MACE

"Lola's having my baby."

Cheers break out in the group.

"I'm taking her back to my cabin to celebrate. You knock, you lose an arm."

Oh Lord, save me. Mace has no filters.

He turns and carries me up the hill to our cabin. He slams the door shut and drops me on the bed. He's on top of me kissing me with hot, urgent, wet kisses. "I love you, babe." His voice is heavy with all the emotion, and it sounds like he's holding back tears.

"I love you too, Mace." I let the tears fall. He kisses them quickly to wipe them away.

His large hand palms the base of my head, and he kisses me again. He's all over me and all around me. His hard cock pokes my belly and his hand traces down the back of my leg to pull my knee up around his hip. Suddenly I have to have him right now. We have to express this with our bodies. There aren't sufficient words to describe how close we are right now.

His hips roll against mine, and my body ignites for him. We peel our clothes off, and I push him to his back. "Mace, you look so damn good up there on that stage. It's not fair how beautiful you are."

"I'm glad you like it. All yours. Forever."

"All mine." I kiss down his chest, and he groans when my lips graze the head of his cock. I slip my lips around the tip, and he squeezes my thighs. I'm just getting my groove on when he pulls me up by my armpits and places me straddling him, his dick smashed in the slick wetness between us.

"Seeing you pregnant is going to drive me wild. I'm going to want to fuck you all the time."

"You pretty much wanted that before too."

"True. Love you, my Lola."

"Love you, my Mace. Forever. Thank you for never giving up on me."

"I never did. Never will. We're living the dream together. Wherever you go, I'm there too. You, me, Seger, and our little girl."

"It could be..." I can't finish my sentence because he lifts me and slams me down on his cock. "Oh." It feels so good. Mace fills me, and I am whole. We make love and celebrate the new life that will be another important link in the eternal chain of the Twist family.

###

Playlist

"All For Love" by Rod Stewart and Bryan Adams
    "Colder Weather" by Zac Brown Band
    "Jealousy" by Natalie Merchant
    "Not Broken Just Bent" by Pink feat. Nate Ruess
    "Porn Star Dancing" by My Darkest Days ft. Ludacris, Zakk Wylde
    "Precious and Few" by Climax
    "Remind Me" by Brad Paisley and Carrie Underwood
    "Remind Me To Forget" by Kygo
    "Senorita" by Camila Cabello and Shawn Mendes
    "Still The Same" by Bob Seger
    "We've Got Tonight" by Bob Seger
    "Wild" by John Legend Meduza Remix

Keep in Touch with Bex

Did you enjoy this book? There's more to come. Sign up to Bex Dane's mailing list on bexdane.com. You'll receive a free ebook and updates on all her new releases.

Printed in Great Britain
by Amazon